"What the hell were you doing standing in the middle of the road like that?" he demanded.

"You could've been killed."

"I wasn't standing in the middle of the road. I was practically on the shoulder, and if you hadn't been driving so fast you would've realized that." Bradlee pulled her hand from his and glared back at him. He was good-looking, tall and broad shouldered, with dark hair and vivid blue eyes.

Eyes that brought a shiver of awareness to Bradlee.

Suddenly she knew exactly who this man was. And the countryside seemed to quiet at the revelation. The wind through the trees, everything stilled around her as she gazed up at him.

After thirty-two years Adam Kingsley had finally come home.

Dear Reader,

When my editor asked me to turn an idea I'd recently pitched to her about a thirty-year-old kidnapping into a three-book series, I was intrigued (and stumped). How could I create three separate mysteries (and three separate love stories) within one big mystery, i.e. the kidnapping? Each book would need its own hero and heroine, its own cast of characters and suspects, and its own (hopefully) satisfying conclusion.

As I considered the possibilities, I began to realize just how many lives would be affected by such a tragedy— the woman whose father was convicted of the crime and the man whose father became a legend for solving the case *(The Hero's Son)*; the kidnapped child's twin brother and a dangerous impostor *(The Brother's Wife)*; and finally, the little girl (all grown-up now) who was in the nursery at the time of the kidnapping and who has been haunted for over thirty years by what she may have seen that night *(The Long-Lost Heir)*.

I hope you've enjoyed THE KINGSLEY BABY series and came to care as much for the characters as I did.

If you've missed any of the books, you can order them through the Reader Service: U.S.: 3010 Walden Ave., P.O. Box 1325, Buffalo, NY 14269. In Canada: P.O. Box 609, Fort Erie, Ont. L2A 5X3.

Happy reading,

Amanda Stevens

The Long-Lost Heir
Amanda Stevens

Harlequin Books

TORONTO • NEW YORK • LONDON
AMSTERDAM • PARIS • SYDNEY • HAMBURG
STOCKHOLM • ATHENS • TOKYO • MILAN
MADRID • WARSAW • BUDAPEST • AUCKLAND

ISBN 0-373-22462-1

THE LONG-LOST HEIR

Copyright © 1998 by Marilyn Medlock Amann

Printed in U.S.A.

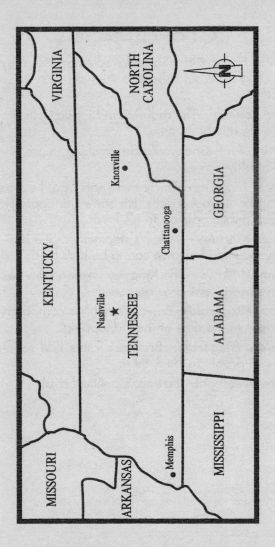

CAST OF CHARACTERS

Bradlee Fitzgerald—She'd loved Adam Kingsley as a child.... Would she love the man he'd become?

David Powers—The real Adam Kingsley. His whole life has been a lie.

Iris Kingsley—She would do anything to preserve the Kingsley power.

Edward Kingsley—Thirty-two years ago, he was trailing badly in the polls. His son's kidnapping swayed public opinion in his favor.

Pamela Kingsley—Adam's stepmother. She has always wanted her own son to be Iris's heir.

Jeremy Willows—The Kingsley stepson who has always been treated as an outsider.

Harper Fitzgerald—Edward's ruthless campaign manager at the time of the kidnapping.

Bradford Fitzgerald—Bradlee's father had serious financial problems back then.

Cotton Weathers—Edward's political rival.

Prologue

Jenny Arpello couldn't shake the premonition that something was wrong. Something wasn't as it should be. In her room adjoining the nursery, she paced nervously, wondering what she should do.

She'd started to say something earlier to Edward Kingsley and his new wife, Pamela, when they'd come up from the fund-raiser downstairs to say goodnight to Edward's three-year-old twins, Adam and Andrew, and again later, when Iris Kingsley, the twins' grandmother, had made her appearance.

But what could she have said? *I have this feeling that something bad is about to happen, but I don't know what. I have this gift, you see. I can sense things. My grandmother had it, too. It runs in my family....*

Jenny could well imagine Iris Kingsley's response to that. She would have looked down her aristocratic nose at Jenny, given her a withering look with those icy blue eyes, and told her in her cultured voice that Jenny's services would no longer be required. Iris

Kingsley would not tolerate a woman she considered mentally incompetent watching over her grandsons.

Jenny was terrified of Iris Kingsley. She was terrified of all the Kingsleys, really. She'd never worked for a family quite as famous, quite as powerful, quite as rich as the Memphis Kingsleys. There had been Kingsley senators, Kingsley secretaries of state, Kingsley diplomats, and, if Edward had his way, the next governor of Tennessee would be a Kingsley.

But Jenny didn't particularly care about politics. Her main concern was keeping her position. She'd only been in the household a month, and in spite of Iris's arrogance, Edward's roving hands, and Pamela's sharp tongue, this was the best job Jenny had landed since graduating from nursing school five years ago.

And the twins were precious—quiet, troubled little Adam, whose soulful eyes tugged at Jenny's heartstrings, and the more rambunctious Andrew, who, at three, was already a charmer.

The boys had lost their mother to cancer a few months ago, and Edward had recently remarried. Jenny suspected that was the reason he was trailing so badly in the polls. His hasty marriage had lent credence to the rumors of his longtime, illicit liaison with Pamela Harrington, a Memphis socialite with two divorces behind her and an eight-year-old son of her own.

At the thought of Jeremy, Jenny winced. Though she loved children, *no one* could consider Jeremy Willows anything but a brat. Thank God he'd been allowed to attend the party downstairs, and Jenny didn't have to put up with him in the nursery tonight. He teased and tormented the twins whenever he thought he could get away with it, and Pamela always took his side.

Outwardly, of course, she made a fuss over Adam and Andrew, smothering the poor little motherless boys with love and attention, but Jenny had seen the way Pamela looked at the twins when she thought no one was watching. She clearly resented Adam and Andrew who, even though they were younger than Jeremy, would someday be the Kingsley heirs.

Opening the door to the nursery, Jenny stepped inside. Moonlight flooded into the room from the French doors that opened onto a balcony overlooking the rear gardens. Out of habit, she checked the latch to make sure it was secure, then crossed the room to close the hallway door. Hadn't she shut it earlier? Had someone been in the nursery without her knowing?

Probably the Fitzgeralds, she decided. Their three-year-old daughter, Bradlee, was asleep in one of the beds, and Mary Fitzgerald couldn't bear to be parted from the little girl for more than an hour or two at a time. And no wonder. The child was incredibly sweet, and her open adoration of little Adam had immediately endeared her to Jenny. Bradlee was the only one who had been able to make him smile since his mother's death.

One by one, Jenny tiptoed passed the little beds. Andrew was sprawled on his back, a smile playing at his lips. Unlike his brother, Andrew hadn't been traumatized by his mother's death. He'd missed her, of course, but like most children, he'd quickly bounced back, readily accepting the affection of anyone willing to give it to him—even his new stepmother. Andrew seemed quite taken with Pamela's excessive beauty and charm, whereas Adam wanted nothing to do with the woman.

Stepping to the next bed, Jenny gazed down at Adam. As usual, he was curled on his side, a pillow clutched to his chest. His eyelids fluttered rapidly in his sleep, as if he were dreaming about something troubling. The premonition Jenny had been experiencing all evening came back full force as she stared down at him, and it was all she could do not to lift the child from his bed and hold him tightly to her breast. Adam was so vulnerable right now. He brought out all her protective instincts.

As Jenny moved on to the third bed, she was surprised to find little Bradlee's eyes open. The child didn't say anything, didn't fuss or fret, just lay there quietly in her bed. Wide-awake. Alert. As if she'd had the same premonition as Jenny.

Jenny shivered. "What's the matter, sweetie?" she whispered. "Did you have a bad dream?"

Bradlee shook her head. She lifted her hand and pointed to Adam's bed.

Jenny smiled. "You're watching out for him, aren't you?"

The little girl nodded, her expression solemn.

Tears stung Jenny's eyes. The bond between the two children was a touching thing to witness.

"Adam's fine." She smoothed back Bradlee's bangs. "He's sleeping. You can sleep now, too. I'll look out for him, okay?"

Bradlee nodded, but her eyes remained vigilant, as if she had no intention of letting herself fall asleep. Jenny tucked the cover around the child's shoulders and then went back to her own room. The uneasiness still hung heavily over her, and she knew she would have a hard time sleeping.

As was her habit, she warmed some milk in the kitchenette next to the nursery, then carried the glass to her bedroom and drank the contents before climbing into bed. Within minutes she fell into a deep slumber.

She didn't hear the nursery door open sometime later nor the soft footfalls that crossed the room. She didn't see the dark shadow standing over her bed nor the empty glass being taken away. She didn't know when the French doors in the nursery were opened nor when the signal was given to someone waiting below in the garden.

Jenny knew nothing until hours later, when a scream awakened her, and she rushed into the nursery to find little Adam Kingsley missing from his bed.

Chapter One

Thirty-two years later

Something was wrong. David Powers knew it as surely as he knew his own name. He frowned, glancing at the stack of phone messages he'd found on his desk after returning from court that morning. Three were from his mother.

Helen Powers never "bothered" him at the office. It was a point of pride with her. In the twelve years David had been with the public defender's office in New York City, he could count on one hand the times his mother had called him at work.

"You're a busy man," she would tell him, ladling another helping of chicken and dumplings—comfort food from her Southern background—onto his plate at their weekly Sunday dinner. "The last thing you need is for me to call you at work and make a nuisance of myself."

David would reply indulgently, if a little impatiently, "I appreciate that. But as I've told you before, if you ever need me, you don't have to be afraid to call the office, okay? Margaret won't bite.''

Actually, he wasn't altogether sure that was true. Margaret Petermen, the receptionist at the P.D.'s office, was a sixty-year-old barracuda who swore profusely, screened calls to a fault, and kept a plaque on her desk proclaiming, I Have One Nerve Left And You're Getting On It.

In spite of his mother's protests to the contrary, David knew Margaret intimidated her. So many people did. His mother was quiet and shy and didn't mix well with others. She liked to keep to herself, rarely even used the phone. Something had to be wrong if she'd gotten up enough courage to brave Margaret's sharp tongue, not once, but three times in as many hours.

He instantly thought of the doctor's appointment she'd had the previous week, the one she'd refused to talk to him about on Sunday. She'd been experiencing severe headaches, and David had insisted she go in for a checkup.

Hesitating for only a second, David picked up the phone and placed the call to Richford, the small town in upstate New York where he'd grown up.

His mother answered on the first ring, as if she'd been sitting by the phone waiting for his call. "David?"

He could hear the tremor in her voice, and his concern deepened. "What's wrong? Are you all right?"

The pause that followed was so long he thought

for a moment the connection had been severed. Then, in a near whisper, she said, "Come home, David. Come home now."

"What's—"

The phone clicked in his ear before he had a chance to finish the question. David stared at the receiver for a second, then hung up and grabbed his briefcase, hurrying out of his cramped, downtown office. He'd never heard his mother sound so distressed. Something was definitely wrong.

"I'm leaving early," he told his secretary, who looked up from her computer in astonishment. "Cancel my appointments for the rest of the day."

"But you have a meeting with Mr. Hollingsworth at four-thirty—"

David swore. He'd forgotten about the interview he had that afternoon at Hollingsworth, Beckman, and Carr, a prestigious Manhattan law firm that had approached him about joining their ranks. A thousand other attorneys would have killed for such an interview, but David was less than enthusiastic. Perhaps if he thought their interest had more to do with his merit and less to do with the fact that J.C. Hollingsworth's daughter, Rachel, was his fiancée, he might have been able to muster a little more excitement.

Besides, he liked working in the public defender's office. He'd made a name for himself here, and every case was a challenge. If he entered the cutthroat world of Hollingsworth, Beckman, and Carr, he had the disturbing feeling he might never be his own man again.

"Make my apologies," he told his secretary without compunction. "Say I was called away on a family emergency. You'd better call Rachel, too. Leave word with her secretary if she's not in. I may not make it back in time for dinner tonight. She's to go without me."

"But Mr. Powers—"

He was out the door and heading down the hallway toward the bank of elevators before his secretary could finish voicing her protest. The doors slid open and Rachel Hollingsworth, dressed in a red Chanel power suit, stepped out. As always, her dark hair was pulled straight back, accenting the perfect angles of her face and the exotic tilt of her gray eyes. She looked elegant, sophisticated, and completely out of place in the institutional surroundings—not at all what she was accustomed to at the Madison Avenue offices of Hollingsworth, Beckman, and Carr.

"Perfect timing!" she exclaimed with a dazzling smile. So dazzling, in fact, that harried passersby in the hallway stopped to stare at her. "I have a one o'clock reservation at Justine's, and I won't take no for an answer."

David glanced at his watch, a functional black Seiko his mother had given to him when he graduated from Columbia. "Sorry, but I've already had lunch, and besides, I'm on my way out."

The smile slipped a bit. "But I came all the way down here just to see you, and you know what traffic is like on Fridays. The least you can do is keep me company while I eat. I need to talk to you about your meeting with Daddy this afternoon—''

"I'm sorry," David said again, placing his hands on her shoulders and bending to give her a perfunctory kiss on her smooth cheek. "I don't have time to talk." Quickly he stepped into the elevator and jabbed the Down button with his thumb. "I'll call you later."

She turned to stare at him in disbelief, her elegant brows arching in icy outrage as the doors slid closed between them. Rachel Hollingsworth was not used to such treatment, and David knew there would be hell to pay later. But right now, he didn't give a damn.

He wondered if he ever had.

A STRANGE CAR WAS parked at the curb in front of his mother's house, and the uneasiness David had been experiencing on the drive up from the city strengthened. He pulled into the driveway, parked his own car, and got out, striding up the flower-lined walkway to the front door. He had his key, but before he could insert it into the lock, the door was drawn back, revealing his mother's careworn face.

She was not a pretty woman, nor had she aged particularly well. Her hair had gone completely gray at a young age, and the deep lines that etched her face had been there ever since David could remember.

She used to tell him fondly that he had gotten his

dark good looks from his father, who had died in Vietnam while David was still a baby. She would show him pictures of a handsome young man in a military uniform, and David would stare at his father's image, trying to find his own features in the stranger's face, but never seeing them there. After a while he quit searching. After a while he stopped asking the questions that always upset his mother so much.

"I came as soon as I could." He stepped into the tiny foyer and closed the door behind him. Over his mother's shoulder, David saw a man in the living room watching them. He looked to be about David's age, mid-thirties, tall and lean, with inquisitive eyes and a solemn expression that matched the somber atmosphere of the house.

David glanced down at his mother. "Are you all right?"

She nodded briefly, her eyes not meeting his. "Come into the living room. There's someone you need to meet."

The stranger came forward to greet him. "My name is Jake McClain. You must be...David." His handshake was firm, his eyes inscrutable as he studied David's face.

Behind him, his mother said, "Mr. McClain is a private investigator from Memphis, Tennessee."

David glanced at her in astonishment. "A private investigator? What the hell is going on here?"

"Maybe I should leave you two alone," McClain

suggested. He looked at David's mother, and his gaze seemed to soften in spite of himself.

She nodded. "Maybe you should." When David started to say something, she put a hand on his sleeve. "Let's sit down."

An eerie sensation crept over David as he sat down on his mother's worn sofa and watched her take a seat in her favorite rocking chair near the fireplace. In the background, the front door closed discreetly as Jake McClain slipped away to allow them privacy.

What the hell was going on? David wondered again, but for some reason, he remained silent. He had a feeling that what his mother was about to tell him was something he just might not want to hear.

Don't ask the question, his legal mind told him, *unless you know the answer.* And right now, he didn't have a clue.

Out of habit, his mother rocked to and fro, her hazel eyes glinting with an emotion David could only call fear. And despair. But it wasn't until they heard Jake McClain's car start up outside and drive away that she broke the silence.

"I've prayed this day would never come," she murmured. "But I somehow knew it would. Secrets always have a way of coming out, my mother used to say. No matter how deeply you bury them."

"Just tell me one thing." David leaned toward her, resting his forearms on his knees. "Does this have anything to do with your doctor's appointment last week?"

Her eyes clouded. "Not really. This day would

have come regardless of what my doctor told me. It just makes things...a bit easier in some ways.''

''What do you mean?''

Without responding, she got up from the rocking chair and crossed the room to the antique walnut wardrobe in the corner. As long as David could remember, she'd kept the key to the wardrobe on a satin ribbon around her neck and only opened it to take out the picture of David's father when he asked to see it.

Once, when he was about seven, she'd caught him trying to pick the lock with a hairpin, and her censure had been so severe he'd never tried again. The contents of the wardrobe, including the photo of his father, had soon been forgotten because that summer David had discovered Little League, and sports had taken over his life.

His mother took the key from her neck and in the almost-preternatural silence of the tiny living room, David heard the distinctive sound as the old-fashioned lock clicked open. Spreading the doors, she withdrew the white, leather-bound photo album he remembered from his childhood and another book he'd never seen before. She retraced her steps across the room, but rather than taking her place in the rocker, she sat down beside him on the sofa and opened the photo album to the picture of his father.

David stared down at the likeness. The photo was black-and-white, but he could tell that his father's eyes were dark, almost black, not blue like David's. The hair was similar, dark and thick with a hint of a wave, but the hairline was different, as was the shape of the face, the nose, the mouth, the high cheekbones that hinted at a Native American heritage. A heritage that did not show in David's own features.

He looked up at his mother and she nodded. "You've always known, I think."

Somewhere deep inside, David felt a brief sense of relief. The truth was about to come out. "He isn't my father, is he?" When his mother shook her head, David asked, "Who was my real father? What happened? Did he run out on you? Refuse to marry you? Did he even know about me?" All the questions he'd wondered about for years came flowing out. It wasn't so much an emotional response as one of curiosity. One of logic. He simply wanted to know.

His mother took a deep, trembling breath. "Your real father was an important man, David. His family was very rich and powerful. Well-educated and cultured. Everything that I'm not."

David took his mother's hand. "You know that's never mattered to me."

Tears glimmered in her eyes. "You've always been a wonderful son, David. I've known from the first you were special. Destined for greatness. I've tried to make sure you had everything you needed to fulfill your destiny."

His mother had scrimped and saved all his life, sometimes working two and three jobs, just so David could have the education and advantages she'd never had. It was a debt he knew he would never be able to repay her.

"Were you and my father ever married?"

She shook her head sadly.

"What happened? The family you mentioned... did they give you a hard time?"

Her hand crept to her throat, and David saw that it was trembling. "They never even knew I existed."

"So it was him," David concluded dispassionately. "It was his decision to have no part of me."

She wavered for a moment, as if considering the truth of his words. Then her gaze dropped to the photograph album still lying open in her lap. She touched the picture lovingly.

"Who is that man?" David asked.

There was another pause, then, "He was my husband."

She couldn't have surprised him more. His mother had always been so quiet and shy. So reserved. To think that she could have had an illicit love affair with one man while married to another—

"Are you saying you were married to this man when my father got you pregnant?"

"My husband was already dead by the time I knew anything about your father." With shaking hands, she lifted the photo album and laid it open on the coffee table in front of them. Then she opened the second album, and a picture of a little boy smiled up at them. With her fingertip, she traced the child's features—the dark eyes, the high cheekbones, the full, smiling lips. He was the spitting image of the man David had always thought was his father.

A cold knot of dread wedged somewhere in David's chest. The whole scenario had taken a turn he hadn't expected, and he wasn't sure what to prepare himself for next. He glanced at his mother, but she was still gazing down at the child's face.

"Who is *he?*" he finally asked.

"My son," she answered softly, so softly David had to strain to hear her.

He gaped at her in shock. "Your *son?*"

Her nod was almost imperceptible. "He and my husband died in a car wreck. My baby was only three years old."

The knot of dread turned to confusion, but David, sensing his mother was teetering on some emotional edge, forced his tone to remain neutral while the world as he knew it started to crumble around him. Before his eyes, the woman who'd raised him had suddenly become a stranger—and his life, a lie. He felt a slight panicky sensation in his chest, not unlike the rare times when he'd been ambushed by his adversary in court.

He checked the date stamped in the right-hand corner of the picture. David had been three years old that year, also. "How could you have two sons the same age? Unless, of course, we were twins, but I don't think that was the case, was it?" He bore not even a passing resemblance to the child in the photograph.

"David." At last his mother looked up at him. A tear spilled down her cheek as she reached out to touch him. Inadvertently he flinched, and pain flashed in her eyes as she let her hand drop to her lap. "I've loved you with all my heart," she whispered. "I couldn't have loved you more if I'd given birth to you."

David sucked in a sharp breath. He'd always known the man in the photograph wasn't his real father; but now, to learn that his mother...wasn't his real mother... What other secrets did she harbor?

He gazed at her for a long moment, then said slowly, "So you're telling me I'm adopted?" When she didn't respond, he demanded, "Why didn't you tell me before? Why keep it from me?" Then another thought dawned on him. "The private investigator who was here—who does he work for? My birth mother?" There was an edge of bitterness in his voice that surprised him.

In his line of work, David had seen the worst life had to offer pass through his office door. He'd made sure he was both mentally and physically tough; he couldn't have lasted in the public defender's office for twelve years if he hadn't been. But the knowledge that his birth mother had given him away wasn't exactly easy to shrug off—even for him.

"Your real mother is dead," Helen Powers told him.

David frowned, unsure how he felt about that revelation. "So who sent the detective? My father?"

"Your grandmother."

David sat back against the sofa, trying to digest all that he'd learned. He had a grandmother somewhere. A grandmother who was trying to find him.

And a father? Brothers and sisters? A whole damned family he'd never known anything about?

"Your mother—your real mother—loved you very much. I'm sure of it. She died when you were only three years old. She had nothing to do with any of this."

"Whose idea was it to give me away, then? My father's?" When she didn't answer, David leaned toward her. "Look, you don't have to be afraid to tell me the rest. You took me in when they didn't want me. You've given me a good life. You're still my mother, and nothing you can say will ever change that."

She squeezed her eyes shut. "You don't know how much I want to believe that," she whispered. She bowed her head, as if overcome with emotion. But when David put his hand on her arm and she looked up, her eyes were clear and resolved.

"I was barely twenty when I lost my husband and my son," she said. "They were everything to me, the only good and decent thing I'd ever known in my life, and then, suddenly, they were gone. Just…gone, as if they'd never existed. I was all alone again. And my arms were so empty. So very empty…"

She took another long breath, as if willing her strength. "Their deaths…did something to me. I couldn't let go. I used to go out to the cemetery and sit by their graves for hours at a time, talking to them and pretending we were all still together. I finally managed to convince myself they weren't really dead, after all. They were just…away somewhere. And one day they'd come back to me.''

A cold chill crept up David's spine. Her eyes were no longer clear, but glazed and distant, as if she'd somehow transported herself back to that time. Back to that dark fantasy.

She took another trembling breath. ''I was working as a waitress in a downtown coffee shop in Memphis. A lot of cops came in there. One of them in particular…he was always so nice to me. Always so kind. He reminded me a little of David.''

David started at the sound of his own name. The movement seemed to bring his mother back for an instant. She nodded absently. ''My husband's name was David. So was my son's. We called him Davey.''

The chill deepened inside David. He'd always known his mother was a little on the fragile side, but the woman who sat before him now seemed almost…lost. She'd named him for her dead husband and son—a husband and son she'd thought were coming back to her.

Was it his imagination or had the temperature in the room suddenly dropped?

David gazed at her with morbid fascination. He told himself he didn't want to hear anything more. Somehow he knew that what she was going to tell him would change his life forever, but he couldn't seem to stop himself from asking, ''What happened with the cop?''

Helen Powers's fingers twisted together in her lap.

"The more he came into the coffee shop, the more I thought he looked like my husband, and the more I started looking forward to his visits. We began seeing each other, and he seemed to know all the places that David and I had gone to, all our favorites songs and movies. I realized later that I'd probably told him these things in all the long talks we had in the coffee shop and at his apartment, but at the time..."

"You wanted to believe that he *was* your husband," David said.

His mother glanced up hopefully. "Then you understand how it could have happened?"

David wasn't sure he understood any of it, but he felt obliged to try. "You were very young, and you'd just suffered a terrible loss. This man preyed on your vulnerability."

She nodded. "He told me he had a child, a son that was the same age as Davey. He wanted me to look after the boy for a few days while he was out of town. He took me to a secluded cabin in the mountains, and told me he'd bring the boy there in a day or two. I was to wait for them. We'd have the time of our lives. He made it sound like an adventure, just the way my David would have."

Her eyes sparkled for a moment in remembrance, then darkened with reality. "I waited in the cabin for two days, and when he finally showed up with the child, I knew right away something was wrong. The boy was crying. He wouldn't stop sobbing. He kept calling for his mommy. It nearly broke my heart."

"And this man, this cop," David said grimly. "What happened to him?"

"He left. He said he'd be back in a week and the three of us could spend a little time together before he had to take the boy back to his family. I knew by then the child wasn't his, but I was afraid to ask too many questions. Afraid of what I might have gotten myself into. So I just didn't think about it. I concentrated all my efforts on the boy. On comforting him. And after a while, he responded. After a while…he clung to me."

David knew what was coming. Like a freight train racing out of control, the truth was about to hit him head-on, and there wasn't a damn thing he could do to stop it.

"What happened when the cop came back?" he managed to ask.

"I don't know." She glanced up, meeting his eyes briefly before turning away again. "I wasn't there. I took the child and…left."

The weight of her words pressed down on David. His chest tightened painfully. "You kidnapped me. That's what you're saying."

She winced as if he'd physically struck her. "Please, try to understand. I loved you from the first moment I laid eyes on you. I couldn't bear the thought of someone taking you away from me. Not again."

"Not *again?* But I wasn't your son. I wasn't Davey."

"But I wanted you to be." Her eyes pleaded with

him for understanding. "I wanted it so badly that I just left that mountain and disappeared with you."

He rubbed his hands over his eyes. It was like the plot of a made-for-TV movie, stranger than any case he'd ever worked on. It couldn't be true, and yet it was. He didn't doubt the validity of her words—not for a second, because he'd always known that something about his life wasn't *right*. "What about my birth certificate?" he asked numbly. "How did you manage that?"

"My father and brother were in and out of prison all of their lives," she said. "I learned things from them. I knew there were ways to get things done."

"So you bought a fake birth certificate." He didn't bother to ask her where she'd gotten the money to do so. He didn't want to know. "All these years, I've thought you were my mother. I've thought you the most caring, the most loyal, the most generous woman I've ever known, when all along you perpetrated the most selfish act I can imagine. You kept me from my real family. Who am I, Moth—" he started to ask, then stopped himself short on the last word. He took a deep breath. "Who am I?"

Without answering, she flipped several pages of the photo album until she came to a newspaper article. The headline read: Kingsley Baby Stolen From Nursery.

A thrill of adrenaline shot through him. *My God,* he thought. Was she trying to tell him *he* was Adam Kingsley?

He glanced up, unable to give voice to the dozens of questions crashing through his head.

"Turn the pages," she said softly.

He flipped the page of the photo album and another headline read: The Search Continues For Adam Kingsley. Still another: Kingsley Baby Found Dead.

David kept turning the pages. He couldn't seem to stop himself. The headlines blurred before his eyes like some strange and horrifying kaleidoscope.

Kingsley Kidnapper Found Guilty.

Cletus Brown Sentenced To Life In Prison.

And then, toward the back of the book, there were more recent articles with headlines proclaiming Cletus Brown's innocence, and the revelation by the real kidnapper, an ex-cop named Raymond Colter, that Adam Kingsley might still be alive.

David turned the pages until he reached the end of the book. Then he sat numbly as the images continued to flash inside his brain. Adam Kingsley. *He* was Adam Kingsley.

Was it possible?

David knew all about the kidnapping. One of his professors in law school had reenacted Cletus Brown's trial in the classroom. David had even been assigned to Brown's mock-defense team.

He thought about that now and wished he could appreciate the irony. He'd gone over every aspect of that case in preparation for the classroom trial. He knew the most minute details of Adam Kingsley's kidnapping, but he hadn't known that *he* was Adam Kingsley.

What a joke, he thought. What a great joke. The best joke he'd ever heard.

So why wasn't he laughing?

The woman who had been his mother less than an hour ago reached out to him beseechingly. When he jerked away from her touch, she put a trembling hand to her lips. "You said I would still be your mother," she whispered. "You said nothing I could tell you would change that."

He stared at her in disbelief. "I had no idea you were a kidnapper when I said that."

"I wasn't the one who took you from your home, David. You have to believe that."

"Oh, I believe it. But in the eyes of the law, you're just as guilty as Raymond Colter. It's called conspiracy. You may not have taken me from the nursery, but you sure as hell didn't return me, either. You let my family think I was dead. You let an innocent man spend over thirty years in prison for a crime you knew he didn't commit. What kind of person could do something like that?" He was being deliberately cruel, but he couldn't seem to stop. He told himself a man shouldn't care about these things. Shouldn't feel all the turbulent emotions churning inside him. He was too logical for that, too indifferent. What happened all those years ago should have no bearing on his life now. He'd been relatively happy until a few minutes ago. Why let what he'd just learned change that?

But it was no use. He couldn't shake the almost-overwhelming sense of betrayal, the cold, hard anger growing inside him. He couldn't forget that his whole life had been a lie.

"God, what a mess," he said, walking to the window to stare out at the street. "You know, of course, that if and when the police get involved, you're going to need an attorney. I can recommend someone—"

"I don't want an attorney," she said in a low voice. "I'm going to go to the police and confess."

David whirled at that. In spite of everything, the notion of her spending the rest of her life in prison was not something he could ignore. He strode across the room to stand over her. "Listen to me. This is a very serious situation. I don't want you to talk to anyone about any of this until you've spoken with an attorney. Not the police, not McClain, no one. Do you understand?"

But she was already shaking her head. "I won't drag this thing out, put you through any more grief than I already have. I'll take my punishment, whatever it is. In the long run, it won't really matter anyway."

Something in her tone alarmed him. "What do you mean, it won't matter?"

She gazed up at him. Pain shimmered in her eyes. "I'm dying, David. I found out last week I have a brain tumor. There's nothing that can be done. But at least now I can make retribution before I go. I can face up to my sins and ask to be forgiven."

David didn't know if that was possible. But he still couldn't help caring for her, grieving for her. She'd been his mother for too long for him to turn his back on her completely. No matter what she'd done. He knelt in front of her. "There must be something they can do for you."

She shook her head. "There's nothing. Just accept it. I have."

"I don't want you to die."

She reached out as if to touch his face, then let her hand fall back to her lap. "I've had a good life, David—far better than I deserved because my happiness was stolen from someone else. Don't grieve for me. Just find a way to get on with your life."

He drew a long, weary breath. "I need some air," he muttered, rising and turning toward the door.

"David." She stood suddenly and caught his arm. "What are you going to do?"

"About what?"

"About...the Kingsleys?"

He shrugged. "I don't know. I guess at some point I'll want to see them."

Fear flashed in her eyes as she clung to him. "Make them come to you, David. Make them come here."

"Why?"

"Don't go back there," she babbled. "Whatever you do, don't go to Memphis."

It was all he could do not to remove her hand from his arm. Suddenly, she had the look of dementia in her eyes. A chill crawled through him as he stared down at her. "Why shouldn't I go to Memphis?" he asked softly, trying not to alarm her any further.

"Because he didn't act alone."

"What? Who are you talking about?"

Her eyes were wide and dazed with fear. David thought he was beyond shock, but to see his mother's face, to realize how close to the edge she really was made him wonder if he could believe anything she'd told him today. What if her illness had made her delusional?

Her grip tightened on his arm. "I heard Raymond talking to someone on the telephone in his apartment one day. I didn't know it then, but they were plotting your kidnapping, David." He could feel her nails dig into his skin through his suit coat. "It was someone in that house who helped him. Someone who was there that night."

It was his turn to grip her arm. He grabbed her shoulders and held her in front of him. "What are you saying?"

Her eyes glowed with an inner intensity—or was it insanity—as she gazed up at him. "Someone in that house paid Raymond Colter to kidnap you. Someone connected to that family wanted you gone. If you go back there now—"

A wave of nausea rose in David's throat. "I don't believe that. Why would my own family hire someone to kidnap me?"

He felt a tremor course through her as she slowly backed away from him. "I don't know. But if you go back there, your life could still be in danger. Whoever hired Raymond Colter to kidnap you might still want to harm you."

IN HER HOTEL ROOM in Cannes, Bradlee Fitzgerald awakened suddenly, an inexplicable finger of apprehension wending its way up her backbone. Getting out of bed, she slipped across the shadowy room and stepped onto the tiny, ornate balcony that overlooked the harbor. An impressive array of yachts, outlined in lights and moored for the night, were strung across the glassy water like diamonds glistening on black satin.

The night was warm and starlit, but the dream that had awakened Bradlee sent an icy chill rushing through her veins. She wrapped her arms around her middle and stared down at the dark waters of the Mediterranean, wondering why the nightmare had returned now, when so many miles and so many years separated her from Adam Kingsley's kidnapping.

Even though she'd only been three years old when it happened, Bradlee had been certain back then that she was somehow to blame for Adam's disappearance; that buried somewhere in the deep recesses of her mind was a clue to his whereabouts, if only she could remember.

The psychiatrist her parents had taken her to after the kidnapping had assured them that her trauma would abate with time. The nightmares would eventually disappear, but perhaps a change of scenery would help.

Her father, Bradford Fitzgerald, had just been hired by one of the top law firms in the city and had no intention of throwing away what promised to be a brilliant future for the sake of a few bad dreams his daughter was experiencing. He refused to leave Memphis, and as a result, her parents had divorced. Her mother had moved with her to Southern California, where Bradlee had grown up.

She'd been twelve years old when she learned the facts behind her parents' breakup, and for a while, Bradlee had blamed herself. The guilt had been so overwhelming that the old nightmares had returned, as they always did in times of distress. Night after night, she'd had visions of a shadow standing over her while she lay helpless in her bed. It was the shadow of someone she knew, someone she trusted, someone she didn't dare give a face to.

It was the shadow of Adam Kingsley's kidnapper.

As a child, she'd seen pictures of Cletus Brown, the man convicted of abducting Adam, but his image hadn't stirred her fear. Not like the dreams had. It wasn't until last year that she'd understood why. After serving thirty-one years in prison, Cletus Brown had been proved innocent, but even when the real kidnapper, Raymond Colter, had come forward and confessed, Bradlee had felt no sense of relief, no sense of justice or peace. Because it wasn't Raymond Colter's shadow she saw in her dreams.

And now the nightmare had come back just when Bradlee thought her life was finally on track. She'd just finished shooting a much-coveted layout for *Charisma,* the L.A.-based fashion magazine for which she freelanced on a regular basis, and she'd been extremely pleased with the results.

The models, the swimsuits, the dazzling Riviera

had all produced a breathtaking effect, and Bradlee knew that Karen Cory Black, the editor-in-chief of the magazine and a close friend, would be ecstatic. There would be other assignments forthcoming, more than enough to keep Bradlee and her two assistants busy throughout the coming year.

But for the next three months, Bradlee was a free woman. No temperamental models to deal with, no frustrating clients to worry about, no impossible deadlines to meet. Just her camera, her backpack, and a Roman holiday she'd been planning for years.

So why the nightmare?

Stress, she told herself as she gazed down at the darkened water. But more likely it was the phone call earlier from her mother. "I heard from your father," she'd said in the formal tone she always used when referring to her ex-husband. "He told me something amazing. Something we both thought you might want to know."

"What is it?" Bradlee asked, wondering if her father was about to plunge into marriage for the sixth time. Or would this be number seven?

Her mother paused dramatically. "They think they've found Adam Kingsley."

Bradlee gasped. Adam had been missing for over thirty years. To think that he might have been found after all this time—

She closed her eyes, conjuring an image of a dark-haired little boy with sad eyes. She hadn't forgotten what he looked like. In all these years, she hadn't forgotten.

"Are they sure this time? I mean, after that terrible business with Andrew's murder and that man claiming to be Adam—how much more can Iris take?"

"Iris Kingsley is strong enough to take just about anything," Bradlee's mother said dryly. "But you're right. I don't think she'd take a chance on being duped by another impostor. The fact that she told your father—or anyone—means she's positive this time. Beyond a doubt."

"So what are they going to do?" Bradlee asked, trying to quiet the flutter of nerves in her stomach.

"Bring him home, I guess. If he wants to come. This is all very secretive, of course. Your father only told me because he thought you should know, considering the way you've always felt about the kidnapping and all. He even suggested you might think about going to Memphis when everything's settled. You know, to see Adam for yourself."

And therein lay the cause of her apprehension, Bradlee thought, shivering as the breeze off the Mediterranean picked up. That was the reason for her nightmare. The prospect of going back to Memphis suddenly terrified her.

You're being silly, she chided herself. So what if she did go to Memphis? There was nothing to be frightened of there. She'd been back dozens of times to visit her father over the years. He still maintained close ties with the Kingsleys, and Bradlee had even stayed at the mansion on occasion, when her presence at her father's place had made things a bit too awkward for whichever new wife he might have had at the time.

Bradlee had gone back last year when it was discovered that Adam might still be alive, and again a few months ago, when his twin brother, Andrew, had been killed. So why was this time any different?

She closed her eyes as a tremor of fear passed through her.

This time was different because if Adam had truly been found, he would have to be warned. If he came back home, his life could still be in danger, and Bradlee might be the only one who could save him.

This time, she couldn't let him down.

Chapter Two

Six weeks later

Bradlee pulled her rented Porsche to the side of the road and got out to walk slowly along the tree-shrouded lane. Up ahead was the entrance to the Kingsley drive, protected by massive iron gates and a guard stationed in the gatehouse who would not allow anyone onto the grounds who hadn't been sanctioned by the family.

The guard didn't worry Bradlee, however. She was expected. For the next few weeks, she would be staying with the Kingsleys, and she marveled at how easily her mission had been accomplished. Almost like fate had stepped in to help her.

As it turned out, her father had impulsively married his current fiancée, and they'd only this week returned from their honeymoon. Bradlee could hardly have imposed on the newlyweds to accommodate her stay, so upon arriving in Memphis, she'd checked into the Peabody Hotel and then phoned Iris Kingsley to pay her respects.

Iris, as Bradlee had known she would, had insisted that Bradlee move out of the hotel and spend the remainder of her vacation at the Kingsley mansion. She would not take no for an answer, and besides, she knew Bradlee was as anxious as the rest of them were to see Adam again. To make sure that he was all right. To see what kind of man he'd turned out to be.

And what kind of man would he be? Bradlee wondered. The child she remembered had been so vulnerable and sensitive, so sweet and caring, but Adam was a man now. The same age as Bradlee. Did he remember her at all? Did he recall the bond the two of them had once shared?

She scoffed at such a notion. They'd only been three years old at the time of his kidnapping. Hardly more than babies. The bond they'd had as children only existed in Bradlee's memory and would have been erased from there long ago if not for Adam's disappearance. The trauma of that night, coupled with Bradlee's misplaced feelings of guilt, had kept that connection alive in her mind, perhaps had even embellished it.

But it didn't really matter if Adam remembered her or not. Bradlee had come here for a purpose, and as soon as her mission was accomplished, she would be free of the past once and for all. Maybe she would even meet someone and fall in love, marry and have the houseful of kids she'd always wanted. Somehow that dream had always eluded her. Somehow her life, in spite of all the advantages she'd grown up with, hadn't turned out quite the way she'd envisioned. Something—some vital piece of the puzzle—always seemed to be missing.

Through the thick copse of trees, Bradlee caught glimpses of the Kingsley mansion, a towering red-brick Tudor that had become legendary throughout the years, especially after the kidnapping. The layout of the house had been featured in every major newspaper in the country, with arrows pointing to the balcony off the nursery where police suspected the kidnapper had gained entrance.

Since Raymond Colter's confession, the authorities had actually learned little more about that night. Colter was spending the rest of his life in prison and had refused to talk beyond his confession. Certain aspects of the case, the hows and the whys, still remained a mystery.

Snapping a zoom lens onto her Nikon, Bradlee lifted the camera to her eye and brought a portion of the house into focus. She was startled to see someone standing on one of the second-floor balconies, although not the one off the nursery because that room faced the rear of the house. But it was in the same wing, and that alone was surprising because Iris had closed off that whole section of the house after the kidnapping. Andrew had been moved into his own room in another wing, and the nanny had been given new quarters on the third floor. Bradlee recalled hearing talk that the nanny had been dismissed sometime later because Iris had never forgiven the woman for allowing her grandson to be kidnapped on her watch.

A chill crept up Bradlee's spine as she continued to stare at the house. Except for Dr. Scott, the psychiatrist her parents had taken her to after the kidnapping, she'd never talked to anyone about her nightmares—about the shadow standing over her bed that night—because she'd never quite brought herself to believe it had really happened. Never quite accepted the notion that someone in the house that night, someone she recognized, had been in the nursery just before the kidnapping.

She'd told herself over and over that even if someone had been in there, it probably had nothing to do with Adam's disappearance. There had been any number of people at the fund-raiser that night, including Bradlee's own parents and her uncle, Harper Fitzgerald, who had been Edward Kingsley's campaign manager. To think that any one of those people might have had something to do with Adam's abduction was ridiculous. Far-fetched. Unbelievable.

And yet the nightmares had persisted. And Bradlee's first inclination on hearing that Adam had been found was to rush here and warn him.

But what would she say? *Someone in your own family may have helped Raymond Colter kidnap you, Adam. Or maybe it was a close friend, someone like my uncle, for instance. Or my father. And whoever it was might not want you to come back. Might do anything to keep you from coming home—*

She would sound like an idiot if she blurted it out in that way. Bradlee knew she would have to be a lot more subtle, because in truth, that shadow might have been nothing more than a traumatized child's imagination; and the nightmare, a product of her guilt. If that were the case, the last thing she wanted to do was taint Adam's homecoming with suspicion.

Bradlee wasn't sure how long she'd been standing at the edge of the lane, camera to her eye, when a sound slowly registered with her and she looked up. A car came tearing around a sharp curve in the road and gathered speed as it straightened, heading directly toward her.

Without thinking, she dived for the ditch and her camera went flying as she rolled down a slight embankment. The driver slammed on his brakes, and Bradlee heard the scream of tires gripping pavement before the car finally came to a halt. A car door slammed and footsteps sounded on the roadway.

Bradlee got to her feet and gingerly brushed leaves off her clothing. A man stood at the side of the road, but she ignored him. She wanted to make sure nothing was broken first. She picked up her camera and examined it.

"Are you all right?" he finally called, a trace of exasperation in his voice—a deep, masculine voice that drew her attention in spite of herself.

"Fine." She held up her camera. "Nothing seems to be broken." She snapped off several shots in the man's direction, and he glared down at her in annoyance. Bradlee started to climb up the embankment, and almost grudgingly, he offered her his hand.

"What the hell were you doing standing in the

middle of the road like that?'' he demanded. ''You could have been killed.''

''I wasn't standing in the middle of the road. I was practically on the shoulder, and if you hadn't been driving so fast, you would have realized that.'' She pulled her hand from his and glared back at him. He was good-looking, tall and broad-shouldered, with dark hair and piercing blue eyes.

Eyes that brought a shiver of awareness to Bradlee.

Suddenly, she knew exactly who this man was, and the countryside seemed to quiet at the revelation. The birds, the wind through the trees, everything stilled around her as she gazed up at him.

After thirty-two years, Adam Kingsley had finally come home.

Something inside Bradlee trembled. She hadn't realized how emotional she would be at this moment. How strong the urge would be to laugh and cry and throw her arms around him.

But he would surely think her crazy, then. Adam Kingsley had lived on in her memory. His kidnapping had shaped her life in ways she couldn't even begin to understand, but to him, she was a stranger. To him, she meant nothing.

Bradlee tried to quiet her racing heart as she stared up at him. He wasn't at all what she'd expected. There was a coldness in his eyes, a hardness in his features that was almost chilling, and it occurred to Bradlee that she'd just traveled thousands of miles for nothing, because here was a man who could take care of himself. Here was a man who would hardly be impressed by her nightmares.

An awkwardness settled between them, and Bradlee turned her attention to his car, a vintage Thunderbird, painstakingly preserved. Not exactly what she was accustomed to seeing a Kingsley drive. "Nice car," she murmured, not knowing what else to say.

"Thanks. But it's hardly in the same league as yours." He nodded toward the black Porsche. "The tabloids must pay you pretty well."

"I beg your pardon."

His gaze dropped to her camera. "I assume you were taking pictures of the Kingsley grounds, hoping to get a shot or two of the long-lost heir."

"I don't work for the tabloids," she said quickly, realizing he'd mistaken her for the paparazzi.

"You're not a photographer?"

"I am a freelance photographer, but I'm not here—"

He cut her off before she had a chance to explain. "The papers all said Kingsley wouldn't be arriving until next week. Aren't you a little early?"

She took a deep breath. "Actually, I think my timing's just about right...Adam."

He lifted one dark brow at that, but didn't bother to deny his identity. "Your paper could have called for an interview, you know. You didn't have to resort to skulking about in the shadows."

"I suppose I could have called," she agreed. "But your identity has been kept a closely guarded secret.

I don't even know your name. I mean...the name you go by.''

"David Powers.'' He held out his hand, and this time, Bradlee was prepared for the shiver along her backbone when he touched her fingers.

"Bradlee Fitzgerald.''

Something flashed in his eyes, a flicker of recognition that brought a brief frown to his brow. "Do I know you?''

He was still holding her hand, and Bradlee felt as if every nerve ending in her body was concentrated in the part of her skin that touched his. She started to tell him who she was then, but another car came racing around the curve, and they moved apart, stepping to the shoulder of the road.

"Well,'' he said, when the car had driven by. "This probably isn't the safest place to stand talking. And I need to get going anyway.'' His gaze lifted toward the mansion. Something in his eyes darkened. "If I were you, I wouldn't let them catch you out here.''

She glanced at him in confusion. "Who?''

"The Kingsleys. I hear they value their privacy above all else.''

Without another word, he turned and walked back to his car.

"Wait! I'm not who you think I am!'' Bradlee called, but he didn't seem to hear her. He got into his car and pulled back onto the road, heading toward the private entrance that would take him to the Kingsley mansion.

Home, after thirty-two years.

Bradlee shivered as she watched him go.

DAVID PARKED HIS CAR in the semicircular drive in front of the mansion and got out to lean against the fender as he stared up at the imposing facade.

Home sweet home, he thought grimly.

He'd thought he'd prepared himself for the grandeur of the Kingsley mansion, but seeing the house in person was far different from viewing newspaper photos of it. The massive structure was awe-inspiring to say the least, and David was hard-pressed to imagine himself ever feeling at home in such a place.

Since he'd learned the truth of his identity six weeks ago, he'd done a lot of research on the Kingsleys. Not much of what he'd learned had been flattering. They were a political family, ambitious, power-hungry, and very often ruthless. Iris Kingsley, the matriarch of the family, was still regarded as the real powerhouse even though she was well into her eighties. Her husband had been a U.S. senator and her son, David's father, had been elected governor of Tennessee not long after the kidnapping. He'd only remained for two terms, however, before retiring from politics, a decision that had created a bitter rift between Iris and him.

Iris had then pinned all her political aspirations on her remaining grandson, but Andrew, from everything David had been able to read about him, had been more interested in racing cars than in running for office.

It was strange to think that he'd had a twin, David reflected. What about the bond identical twins were supposed to share? Why hadn't he known about Andrew? Why hadn't he sensed his brother's death?

Why didn't he have memories of this house? Of the people inside?

David felt nothing as he stared up at the mansion—nothing but a dark premonition that there were other secrets yet to be revealed. And that was why he was here. To find out if everything Helen Powers had told him was true. *Someone in that house paid Raymond Colter to kidnap you. Someone connected to that family wanted you gone.*

But why? What had he done at the age of three to make someone want to get rid of him? Why him, and not Andrew?

David pushed himself away from his car and started up the steps to the entrance.

A uniformed maid answered the door. The guard at the gate had called the house and alerted them that he was here—a week earlier than expected. David wouldn't have been surprised if they'd turned him away, told him to come back next week as planned, but evidently such had not been the case. The guard had opened the gates, looking at David with new respect as he drove through.

The maid wore an almost-identical expression. For a moment, she appeared speechless, then she stammered, "Please, come in, Mr. Kingsley. Your father is waiting for you in the library."

"Thank you," David said cordially. "But my name is Powers. David Powers."

The maid looked flustered for a moment, as if she didn't quite know what to do. From the top of the stairs, a woman's voice said, "It's all right, Illiana. I'll show...Mr. Powers into the library."

The woman who slowly descended the stairs looked to be in her early fifties, but she was dressed much younger, in a short yellow skirt and silk blouse that flattered a still-slender figure. Her hair was very blond, smooth and sleek, just touching her shoulders. As she crossed the foyer toward him, a cloud of expensive perfume enveloped David. When she held out her hand, the glitter of diamonds almost blinded him.

On closer scrutiny, she was older than he'd originally thought, David realized. The exotic tilt of her eyes and the almost unnatural tautness of her skin were both dead giveaways as to just how she'd maintained her youthful appearance.

"I'm Pamela Kingsley," she said, taking his hand very briefly before releasing it. She studied him curiously. "So you're Adam."

"I prefer to be called David," he said. "At least for the time being."

Something flashed in her eyes—an emotion David couldn't quite fathom. She smiled slightly. "Of course. I'm sure we'll all need time to adjust."

In spite of the age difference and coloring, she reminded him a little of Rachel, though for the life of him he couldn't figure out why. It wasn't a comparison he particularly wanted to explore.

He wondered briefly what Rachel was doing at that moment. It was late afternoon, so she was probably having drinks with a client, maybe making dinner plans. She would be expecting a call from him later, and explanations as to why he'd decided against pursuing a career at Hollingsworth, Beckman, and Carr, why he'd taken a leave of absence from his job, and why he'd suddenly left town without telling her where he was going. His were hardly the actions of a loving and devoted fiancé, but then theirs was hardly that type of relationship. Neither one of them had any illusions in that regard.

Pamela lifted a diamond-encrusted hand to her throat. "As Illiana said, Edward is waiting for you in the library. I'm sure you're anxious to meet him."

"Yes, I am," David agreed, glancing around his opulent surroundings.

His eyes lit on a painting in the foyer. He was sure it was a Renoir, but he couldn't begin to guess how much it might have cost. He realized once again that all his research, all his soul-searching in the last six weeks hadn't prepared him for the scope of the Kingsleys' wealth. Even the Hollingsworth estate in Greenwich, Connecticut, couldn't compare to this.

He glanced back at Pamela Kingsley, and her eyes narrowed on him. She smiled at him coolly, as if to say, *You don't fool me. I know exactly why you're here.*

She turned on her heel. "This way."

As she led him down a corridor lined with more paintings, David asked, "What about Mrs. Kingsley?"

"I'm Mrs. Kingsley," she replied, glancing over her shoulder. "I'm Edward's wife."

"I meant the other Mrs. Kingsley. My... grandmother."

Pamela paused before a set of ornate doors with what appeared to be gold handles. "Unfortunately, Iris is feeling under the weather. She's taken to her bed for a few days. She was hoping to be recuperated by the time you arrived, but since you came early..." She trailed off, but her meaning was clear. She didn't appreciate unexpected guests or surprises.

"I'm sorry to hear that," David said. "I was hoping to meet her."

"Perhaps in a day or two." Pamela opened the double doors and stepped inside the library.

David followed her. The room was large, and like the rest of the house he'd seen so far, lavishly decorated with Persian rugs, priceless artwork, and heavy antique furniture that gave the room an air of oppression. For a moment, he thought no one was there, but then his gaze shifted and he saw a man standing at the French doors, staring out into the garden.

He gave no indication of having heard them come in, and Pamela said, rather impatiently, "He's here, Edward."

The man turned at that and slowly crossed the room toward them. He was tall and heavy-set, with hair that had gone completely white and faded blue eyes that seemed to have a hard time focusing. David searched his face, looking for his own features, but Edward Kingsley was as much a stranger to him as the man in the photograph, the man he'd always thought was his father.

"So you're finally here." Edward cleared his throat, as if not knowing what else to say. "Welcome home."

The moment was excruciatingly awkward. It was apparent to David that Edward was not an overly demonstrative man, nor one particularly comfortable with emotion. Perhaps none of the Kingsleys were. The house, while beautiful, was very formal and exuded little warmth.

Finally, they shook hands.

"Well," Edward said. "Perhaps we should sit down."

He took a seat near the fireplace, and David sat down on the leather sofa. Pamela moved to the bar. "Would anyone care for a drink?" She turned and stared pointedly at her husband.

Edward looked as if he could use a good stiff belt, but instead he murmured, "Perhaps a Perrier."

Amusement glinted in Pamela's eyes. "And what about for you...David?" Somehow she made the slight hesitation before his name sound derisive.

"I'll have the same," he said, glancing at Edward. The man was looking a little green around the gills, and when Pamela handed him his drink, David noticed that Edward's hands were shaking. Judging by the bags under his eyes and the slackness of his jaw, David guessed that Edward hadn't been on the wagon for long. And his loving wife didn't appear to be offering much in the way of moral support. She perched on the arm of her husband's chair and savored her own drink—a vodka martini.

"Mother tells me you're a lawyer," Edward said.

"Yes. I work in the public defender's office in New York."

Pamela raised an eyebrow at that. "A public defender? Imagine that, Edward."

"Where did you go to school?" Edward asked, ignoring his wife's sarcasm.

"Columbia."

He nodded in appreciation. "Excellent school."

"Of course, Edward graduated from Harvard," Pamela said, running a fingernail around the rim of her glass. "So did my son, Jeremy."

"Excellent school," David said, meeting her gaze. She had the grace to blush slightly and glance away.

Just then, the maid, Illiana, appeared in the library doorway. "I'm sorry to interrupt, Mr. Kingsley, but Mrs. Kingsley would like to see her grandson, that is, Mr. Powers, upstairs in her sitting room."

"Out of the question," Pamela said, rising. "She's in no condition to be receiving visitors."

Illiana managed to look both meek and triumphant at once. "Mrs. Kingsley said to tell you she's feeling much better. And she would like to see Mr. Powers at once."

"Very well," Edward murmured, also getting to

his feet. He set his untouched Perrier aside and turned to David. "We'd better humor her. Mother can be...difficult when she doesn't get her way. Besides, she's been waiting a long time for this moment. We all have."

It was the closest thing to emotion he'd shown since David arrived, and in spite of himself, David felt his own emotions stir. But he quickly reminded himself why he'd come here. All he wanted was the truth, and he damn well would have it. Thirty-two years of his life had been stolen from him, and though he could never get it back, he could at least have the satisfaction of knowing *why*.

He followed Illiana out of the library and back down the corridor to the curving staircase. At the top, she led him to a suite on the south side of the house and knocked discreetly on the heavy wooden door. A voice called, "Come in," and Illiana opened the door and ushered David inside.

She didn't wait to make introductions, but instead beat a hasty retreat, closing the door firmly behind her. David stood for a moment, glancing around. This must be a sitting room, he surmised, since he didn't see a bed. Done in shades of green and gold, the room was surprisingly warm and a welcome respite from the somber atmosphere of the library.

An elderly woman with gleaming white hair reclined on a green silk chaise near the windows, her legs hidden by a blanket and her arms and shoulders covered by an ivory quilted robe.

A younger woman sat in a striped chair near the

chaise. She got up when David entered the room and headed toward the door. "You two will want to be alone," she murmured, deliberately keeping her head lowered as she neared David. He had only a brief impression of brown hair, darker brown eyes, and a slender, jeans-clad body before the woman breezed past him and slipped out the door.

Then it hit him who she was. He spun toward the door, but she was already gone, and David turned back to face Iris Kingsley. Her piercing blue eyes— so like his own—raked him with unabashed curiosity, and he could hardly do anything other than cross the room and greet her.

"So you're Adam," she said in a soft, Southern drawl. "It's funny, but you don't look as much like Andrew as *he* did. I'm not sure I would have known you." When David remained silently puzzled, she added, "You do know you had a twin brother?"

"Yes, I read that somewhere," he said, determined not to succumb to the woman's charisma. Even at her age, Iris Kingsley was still a powerful woman. It was hard not to react to her presence.

"He was murdered a few months ago by a man claiming to be you."

"I read that, too. I'm sorry. It must have been a difficult time for you."

"There's only been one other time in my life that equaled the sorrow." She didn't elaborate further, and David could only speculate what that other time had been. His kidnapping? Had Iris Kingsley grieved for him as she had Andrew? Somehow it was hard to imagine this regal, arrogant stranger weeping for anyone.

She waved her hand toward the chair the younger woman had vacated, and after David had sat down, she said, "Tell me about yourself, Adam."

"David," he corrected. "I really don't feel as if I'm Adam Kingsley. Not yet, at least."

"But you are. The DNA tests were conclusive." The tests had been Iris's idea, but David had readily complied. He wouldn't even agree to meet with the Kingsleys' attorneys until he knew for sure that everything his mother—Helen Powers—had told him was true.

She'd told him the truth about his birthright: He *was* Adam Kingsley. The tests had proved that. But what about the other matter? Had someone connected to this family arranged the kidnapping?

His homecoming had hardly been met with open arms. Edward had been awkward and uneasy with him, Pamela cold and distrusting, and now Iris, cordial but wary. It occurred to David that all three of them had been in the house the night of his kidnapping, but what had any of them had to gain from his disappearance?

"I heard about Helen Powers," Iris was saying. "It was a brain tumor, I understand."

David nodded, surprised to find the grief still as sharp and painful as it had been four weeks ago. "It was sudden. She went far more quickly than her doctors had predicted."

"Perhaps her death was a blessing," Iris murmured. She glanced up at him. "I'd be lying if I said I was sorry. That woman caused this family immeasurable grief. I can feel no remorse that she's gone."

"I can understand that," David said. "But believe it or not, she was a good mother to me. She gave me a good home."

"I'm glad of that. I'm very thankful you were taken care of. You don't know how many nights I've lain awake wondering—" She broke off, as if overcome by emotion. But then, with an effort, she lifted her chin and blinked away the glitter in her blue eyes. "I can't imagine how difficult this must be for you. It's difficult for all of us, really, even though it's also a time of great joy. This family has been through a lot in the past few months. If we seem…subdued, you'll have to forgive us. Our emotions are a bit ragged at the moment."

"I understand."

"You must have so many questions," Iris said.

"Yes, I do." David leaned forward. "For starters, who was that woman who was in here earlier?"

Iris looked only mildly surprised by the question. David had the distinct impression that not much would ruffle her. "You mean Bradlee? She's staying with us for a while. The Fitzgeralds have been friends of ours for years."

A friend of the family. That certainly explained the Porsche, David thought dryly.

"Have you two met?" Iris inquired.

"As a matter of fact, we have. She was outside

the gate earlier when I drove in. She led me to be-lieve she was a tabloid photographer, staking out the grounds to get a picture of me."

Iris smiled. "That sounds like Bradlee. I'm sure the deception wasn't deliberate, but she has a way of getting herself into situations she can't seem to get out of." She paused for a moment and the smile faded. "Actually, the two of you have met before."

David glanced at her curiously.

Iris nodded. "Bradlee was in the nursery with you and Andrew the night you were abducted."

David looked at her in shock. From studying the case in law school and more recently, he'd known there was another child in the room that night, a little girl the same age as he and Andrew. But he couldn't recall ever having read her name.

Bradlee Fitzgerald. The name fit the mental image he had of a rich and pampered debutante. A friend of the Kingsleys.

"The two of you were very close back then," Iris was saying. "You were devastated by your mother's death, and Bradlee tried to take care of you. We used to call her your little guardian angel. We were all so very worried about her after your...after the kidnapping."

"Why?" David asked.

Iris adjusted the blanket over her legs, as if she'd grown suddenly cold. "The kidnapping deeply af-fected her. She had nightmares for months afterward. Her parents took her to a psychiatrist who finally suggested a change of scenery might help. That was all Mary—her mother—had to hear. She uprooted the child, tore her away from her father, her friends and family, and moved her to Los Angeles. That's where Bradlee grew up.''

David wanted to ask what Bradlee was doing back in Memphis, back in the Kingsley mansion, but he felt his interest might be a little too obvious.

Iris said, "Listen to me go on like this. You must be anxious to get settled in. I've put you in the west wing. It's very quiet, and there's a lovely view of the gardens. You won't be disturbed.''

David stood, realizing he'd been dismissed. He stared down at her for a moment, uncertain what to say. Finally, he shrugged. "It was nice meeting you."

Iris inclined her head slightly. When he turned and started toward the door, she said "Adam?"

He glanced back. She made no effort to correct herself, but instead said, "Welcome home, my dear."

Her words were warmly spoken, but there was something in her eyes that chilled David just the same.

Chapter Three

Bradlee was surprised to find her father and his young new wife in the library that evening having predinner cocktails with Edward and Pamela. Bradlee moved across the room to accept her father's embrace and a cool peck on the cheek from her new stepmother, a woman who was probably ten years younger than Bradlee.

Crystal Fitzgerald was tall, blond, extraordinarily thin and extraordinarily buxom, and she'd dressed accordingly—in a black jersey dress that clung to all the right places. Bradford Fitzgerald couldn't keep his hands off her, Edward couldn't keep his eyes off her, and Pamela couldn't quite pull off the air of indifference she'd tried to assume for the evening. Even at her age, she wasn't used to being upstaged in her home by another woman—unless, of course, it was Iris Kingsley herself.

But Iris wasn't going to make an appearance tonight. She was still under the weather and had decided against coming down for dinner. The only person missing from the scene was Adam—David, Bradlee mentally corrected herself.

"Darlin', don't leave," her father said when Bradlee started to drift away from the group. He kept a protective arm around his new wife, drawing her close. "I haven't seen you in ages, and besides, you and Crystal need to get acquainted."

"I'm not going far, just to freshen my drink," Bradlee told him, holding up her half-empty wineglass. But in truth, she wanted nothing more than to escape. The atmosphere in the library was stifling, and if she stayed one minute longer, Bradlee knew she was apt to tell her father exactly what she thought of him. *Grow up, already!* she wanted to scold him. *Do you have any idea how ridiculous you look with that…child!*

Maybe you're just jealous, a little voice inside her taunted. Her father found love—if you could call it that—at the drop of a hat while Bradlee couldn't seem to find it at all. She hadn't had a serious relationship in years.

The French doors had been left open to the mild September night, and Bradlee walked over to stand in front of them. She closed her eyes, enjoying the breeze blowing in from the garden. By day, the weather was still hot and muggy, but the evenings brought a hint of autumn to the air. She breathed deeply, inhaling the scent of falling leaves and fading roses.

When she turned around, she saw that David had come into the room. Something stilled inside Bradlee. She caught her breath at the sight of him. He was very handsome—not in a smooth and polished way as Andrew had been—but tough and capable and unmistakably masculine. It was hard to remember that this man had once been a sensitive, vulnerable three-year-old whom Bradlee, in her own childish way, had tried to protect.

She watched him walk across the room to greet Edward and Pamela, who in turn introduced him to Bradlee's father and to Crystal. She saw his gaze flash to the low neckline of Crystal's dress, and a wave of resentment swept over Bradlee. Honestly, did every man in the room have to ogle the woman?

At that moment, David looked up and caught her eye, and Bradlee suddenly became very aware of the way *she* looked—her loose, windblown hair, the simplicity of her white dress, the fact that she wasn't quite as thin as Pamela or as curvy as Crystal. She was, in fact, quite ordinary and she'd never been more aware of it than at that moment.

Someone must have told David that the Kingsleys always dressed for dinner because he was wearing an elegant gray suit with a white band-collared shirt underneath. He looked sophisticated and cosmopolitan, very much at home in the Kingsley mansion.

After a few moments, he excused himself from the group and crossed the room to join Bradlee. She tried to calm her racing heart by sipping her wine and looking nonchalant.

"The Porsche should have been a dead giveaway," he said.

Startled, Bradlee glanced up at him. "I beg your pardon?"

"You're not a photographer. You're a friend of the Kingsleys," he said, almost accusingly.

"Yes, but I'm also a photographer, just like I said. And in a way, I *was* waiting for you."

"I didn't tell anyone I was coming today. How did you know?"

She shrugged. "A lucky guess?"

One dark brow rose at that. "Why were you waiting for me out there?"

Bradlee hesitated. Now was the time to tell him about the shadow in her nightmares and about her suspicions. About the real reason she'd come back to Memphis. But what if the dream was only that? What if the shadow was her own personal version of the bogeyman? He would think she was an idiot, and at the moment, Bradlee wasn't so sure he would be wrong.

When she didn't answer right away, he said, "I think I understand. Iris told me you were the little girl in the nursery the night I was kidnapped. I guess it's only natural you'd be curious about me."

A wistful smile touched Bradlee's lips. "You don't know how often I've thought about you over the years, wondered where you were, if you were all right. I never could believe you were dead."

The sincerity of her words seemed to touch him. Something that looked almost like gratitude flashed in his eyes before he quickly masked the emotion by lifting his drink to his lips. "Iris mentioned we were close back then. She said they called you my 'little guardian angel.' " He gave her a sidelong glance.

"So I've been told." Bradlee couldn't help smiling. He was at least six inches taller than she, with broad shoulders and a trim, muscular physique. To think that she had once considered herself his protector was almost comical.

"Were you also friends with my brother? Did you know Andrew?"

Bradlee's amusement faded. She wasn't at all sure she wanted to be the one to tell him about Andrew. His brother had been charming and charismatic, but he'd also had a dark side. A weak side. Did that darkness run in the family?

"My mother and I moved to California when I was still small. I used to come back to visit my father every so often, and sometimes, if it wasn't convenient for me to stay with him, he'd arrange for me to stay here. I knew Andrew, but we weren't especially close. We were two very different people. He liked to live life on the edge, and I was always more of a homebody. A wallflower."

"You didn't like him?"

"I didn't say that. He was very charming. I liked him a lot, but I don't think I ever really knew him." She paused, choosing her words carefully. "Sometimes I've wondered if the kidnapping made him the way he was. If he was attracted to danger because of his guilt."

"What did he have to feel guilty about?"

Bradlee lifted her gaze to his. "Because you were the one who was kidnapped and he wasn't."

David's own gaze darkened. "Sounds like you knew him pretty well."

"Not really. I just know myself."

"*You* feel guilty about what happened? Why?"

She glanced away. "You said it yourself. I was your guardian angel and I let you down."

"You were just a kid, a baby. It wasn't your fault I was kidnapped."

Bradlee tucked a strand of hair behind one ear. "Intellectually, I know that, of course. But emotionally…" She trailed off. "It never went away, you know. Every year on the anniversary of the kidnapping, some newspaper or magazine would do a feature on you. The publicity tapered off after a while until only the big anniversaries were noted—ten years, fifteen years, twenty-five years. But it didn't matter how much time went by, because every time I saw pictures of you it would all come back. All the emotions. All the terror and the grief and the guilt." She spread her hands helplessly. "Everything."

"But you were only three years old." He looked as if he didn't quite know what to say to her. As if he wasn't terribly comfortable with what she was telling him.

Bradlee groaned inwardly. She had a way of blurting out her true feelings without thinking through the consequences. What must he think of her—a woman who'd practically admitted she'd carried a torch for him since she was three years old?

He probably thinks you're pretty pathetic, that's what.

She refrained from slapping her forehead. Instead, she took a long swallow of wine.

David stared down at her, not sure what to say. He'd never met a woman as open about her feelings as Bradlee. It made him a little uncomfortable. He was used to a lot of game-playing, especially in Rachel's social circles, and he'd gotten pretty good at it. He wasn't sure how to handle this honesty thing.

Could she really have remembered him after all these years? Remained so distraught about his kidnapping? It was hard to believe. Thirty-two years had gone by, and they'd been so young at the time. *He* couldn't remember. Why would she?

Maybe this was some kind of game, too, he decided. Maybe Bradlee Fitzgerald had her own agenda, but as David stared down at her, he was hard-pressed to believe it, maybe because he didn't *want* to believe it. It felt good to know that someone had cared about him all these years, wondered about him. Remembered him. The Kingsleys were all so aloof, but Bradlee seemed truly glad he'd been found. He saw the sincerity in her eyes every time he looked at her.

Which happened to be a lot, he acknowledged.

Of the three women in the room, she was easily the most appealing, although David suspected she wouldn't have believed him if he told her so. Her attractiveness wasn't as overt as Crystal's or as studied as Pamela Kingsley's, but instead it had a way of sneaking up on you and catching you by surprise.

She wasn't tall like Rachel, nor as polished and sophisticated, though their backgrounds were probably very similar. But she was trim and athletic-looking, and the freckles across her nose gave her a healthy, girl-next-door quality that David found surprisingly seductive. She wasn't his type, and yet he couldn't stop looking at her.

He saw her frown as she stared across the room at her father and his new wife, and David wondered what she was thinking, what she was feeling.

"Does it bother you?" he found himself asking. "Your father's new marriage?"

"I should be used to it. This is number seven." Her smile was ironic, but she didn't bother to hide the pain in her brown eyes. She shrugged. "Over the years, as his bank account has grown, his wives have gotten progressively younger and more beautiful. Crystal is his reward for managing to keep the Kingsley account at the firm after that nightmare with Victor Northrup last spring."

"You mean Northrup's involvement in Andrew's murder?" When she glanced up at him in surprise, David shrugged. "I've done my homework. Actually, my mother's brother was mixed up in Northrup's scheme. That's how Jake McClain eventually found me."

Bradlee nodded. "Yes, I know. Victor Northrup was the managing partner at Northrup, Simmons, and Fitzgerald. He was the Kingsleys' attorney, as well as a close personal friend. When it came out that he'd helped engineer Andrew's murder so that he could pass off an impostor as Adam Kingsley—as you—everyone thought the firm would go under. The publicity was horrendous, but somehow my father managed to convince Iris to remain with the firm, and she gave him the Kingsley account. Other clients followed her lead and my father is now a hero. And thus, Crystal.''

A man had come into the room, and David nodded toward the doorway. ''Who's that?''

Out of the corner of his eye, he saw Bradlee stiffen when she saw the newcomer. He was fortyish-looking, tall and reed-thin, with a receding hairline and features that were distinctively unattractive.

''That's Jeremy Willows,'' she said, barely suppressing a shudder. ''Your stepbrother.''

David watched as Jeremy crossed the room to Pamela and the two of them drifted away from the others. Pamela said something to her son, who listened intently, then lifted his head and looked directly across the room at David.

David inclined his head slightly, but Jeremy showed no reaction, made no move to cross the room and welcome David home. Instead, he turned and left the room as quickly as he'd entered it.

''What was that all about?'' David muttered, half to himself.

''With Jeremy, it's anybody's guess. He's always been…different.''

''Different?''

Bradlee grimaced. "Very different. He has a huge chip on his shoulder because he's always been treated like an outsider here—even after all this time. Edward and Pamela were married just a few weeks before your kidnapping, and maybe that's why Iris could never accept Jeremy. Maybe he was a painful reminder to her of the real grandson she'd lost. I don't know what her reasons were, but I guess I can understand Jeremy's resentment. And Pamela's."

"Does he still live here, in this house?" David asked.

"Yes, that's the curious part. You'd have thought he would have moved out a long time ago, but he's stuck it out here. I've often wondered if he's still been hoping Iris will change her mind about him. Make him her heir." Bradlee paused. "I don't expect he was all that thrilled to hear you'd been found."

When David didn't respond, Bradlee glanced up at him, her expression worried. "Look, I know this is going to sound strange, but…" Impulsively, she laid her hand on his arm. Was it his imagination, or could he feel the warmth of her skin through his jacket? "Be careful, okay? I don't want to ruin your homecoming, but…" She trailed off again, letting her hand drop from his arm as she glanced away.

"What are you trying to say?" A sudden uneasiness prickled the back of his neck. Her voice had taken on an ominous tone, and David couldn't help but remember why he'd come back here; the secrets he hoped to uncover.

"Just be careful," she said, and with that, she turned and walked away.

THAT NIGHT BRADLEE had the nightmare again. When she awakened, she lay in bed for a long time, staring at the shifting patterns on the ceiling and straining to recall the nuances of the dream—some little detail that would reveal the identity of the shadow standing over her bed. But as always before, the shadow remained elusive, just out of her sight, taunting her and defying her to remember.

Bradlee got up and drew on her robe. Opening the door to the hallway, she peered out. It was well after midnight, and no one was about. Slipping out of her room, she closed the door softly behind her, then paused for a moment to get her bearings. Even though it had been years since she'd been in the part of the house where the nursery was located, Bradlee knew exactly how to get there.

Following a maze of corridors from one wing of the house to the next, she at last found herself outside the door to the nursery. Pausing with her hand on the handle, she willed her heart to stop racing. But it was no use. It beat against her rib cage like a trapped bird, and Bradlee felt herself weakening, her courage deserting her. She didn't want to go into that room.

Coward, she chided herself. *You're not three years old anymore. There's nothing in there to be afraid of.*

After a moment, she grew calmer. She closed her

eyes, trying to recall the details of the nursery, but the room itself was only a hazy memory. What would she find inside? Would the room bring that night rushing back to her? Would she remember the identity of the shadow?

Or would she discover that her nightmares had been nothing more than a manifestation of her terror?

There was only one way to find out. She pushed down on the handle, but it refused to yield to the pressure. The room was locked.

Bradlee wasn't sure whether to be relieved or disappointed. It was possible that the nursery held memories she didn't *want* to recall.

She turned to go, but a shadow in the hallway stopped her cold. Bradlee gasped, her hand flying to her heart. For a moment, she thought her nightmare had come to life, but then she recognized who it was and let out a long breath of relief.

"David! You scared me half to death."

He walked toward her in the dimly lit hallway. "What are you doing here?"

"I might ask you the same thing." Even as he drew closer to her, his face was still shadowed with an emotion Bradlee couldn't define. It occurred to her suddenly that even though David Powers and Adam Kingsley were one and the same man, he was still very much a stranger to her. She had no idea what his life had been like. How he'd been raised. What kind of person he'd turned out to be.

She shivered, watching him.

"I came here to see the nursery." He reached past

her to rattle the handle. "Who has the key, do you think?"

Bradlee shrugged, her heart still pounding painfully inside her. "The staff, I guess. Iris, for sure."

He glanced down at her. "Any chance she'd let us borrow it?"

Bradlee shrugged again. "I don't know. After the kidnapping, she wouldn't let anyone come near this room. Now, though, maybe her feelings have changed."

David turned to stare down at her. "Are you saying you haven't been in here since that night?"

"I've wanted to, but..."

He shook the handle again, though they both knew it was futile.

Another thought came to Bradlee. "How did you know where to come? This house is a maze of corridors."

It was his turn to shrug. "Don't ask me. I somehow just knew."

The comment was more telling than he realized. For some reason his words were more important to Bradlee than all the other proof of his identity, including the DNA test results and his resemblance to Andrew. His knowing how to find the nursery was concrete evidence to Bradlee that he really was Adam. A doubt she hadn't even known she harbored flitted away, and all her feelings for him—the bond they'd once shared—came rushing back. She wanted to put her arms around him and tell him how glad she was that he'd been found, how happy she was that he'd come home, but she knew such an action wouldn't be appropriate. Not yet, at least.

"So what do you suggest we do now?" he asked. "Short of breaking in."

She couldn't help smiling. "That would be a first for us, you know. I've been told we used to try and break *out* of the nursery every chance we got. Andrew could manage it, but you and I always got caught."

"Why was that?"

She grinned. "Because you were a slowpoke, and I always had to wait for you."

He gave her a bemused glance. "So it was my fault, was it?"

"If you must know, Adam, you were a bit of a chicken back then."

The moment she said his name, something changed. The playfulness between them disappeared, and Bradlee felt her awareness of him deepen. He stared down at her, his expression enigmatic.

"So you took care of me," he said softly. "And you always waited for me."

"Yes. I always waited for you, no matter how long it took."

She caught her breath at the look on his face. A look that told her he just might kiss her if she would let him.

Slowly he lifted his hand to skim his knuckles across her cheek. "Why?"

Because you were my best friend, she thought. *My*

soul mate. Back then, I loved you more than anyone in the whole world.

But she knew it was impossible for three-year-olds to have such feelings, that the publicity and interest in the kidnapping through the years had not only kept her emotions alive, but had embellished them. She knew what she was feeling at this moment wasn't real, and so Bradlee said nothing. But her heart quickened at the gentleness of his touch, at the dark intensity of his gaze. She tried to let him know, without saying the words, that if he wanted to kiss her, she wouldn't push him away.

He dropped his hand from her face and took a step back from her. Disappointment, keener than any Bradlee could imagine, ripped through her.

"It sounds to me as though we were quite a pair back then," he said softly.

Bradlee drew a long breath. "We were, Adam. We really were."

Chapter Four

Bradlee was already seated at the breakfast table when David came down the next morning. Their gazes touched briefly before he glanced away to greet the others at the table—Edward, Pamela, Jeremy and Iris, who had insisted on coming down this morning, even though she still looked pale and listless.

The atmosphere at the table was cordial, but Bradlee couldn't understand the lack of warmth. Adam had been missing from their lives for over thirty years. Why were they not gushing with gratitude that he'd been returned to them?

Maybe it was because of the impostor, she thought. The man who'd claimed to be Adam. Iris—the whole family—had opened their arms and their hearts to him, only to find that he wasn't Adam, after all; and that he'd been involved in Andrew's death.

The Kingsleys had given the impostor the welcome that should have been David's. On some level Bradlee could understand the family's wariness, even though they had proof that David was Adam, but she couldn't help resenting their attitude toward him just the same. She wanted to grab them and shake them until their formal facades crumbled away, exposing their true emotions.

She caught David's eye and he smiled slightly, as if he knew exactly what she was thinking. His shrug was almost imperceptible, but it spoke volumes.

"So how long are you planning to stay with us?" Pamela asked. Her makeup was flawless, even so early in the morning, and her hair had been pulled back and fastened neatly with a gold clip. A few wispy tendrils remained at her temples, covering the scars left by the surgeon.

Edward, still wearing pajamas and a silk dressing gown, frowned at his wife across the table. "For God's sake, the boy just got here. Leave him alone."

"Don't scold me as if I'm a child."

"Then stop acting like one."

Iris, seated at the head of the table and looking fragile but regal in a black tailored suit and ropes of pearls, set down her delicate porcelain cup with a clatter. "Stop this, both of you. I will not have this petty bickering at my breakfast table."

"All I said was—" Pamela began, but a sharp look from Iris silenced her.

As if to cover his mother's embarrassment, Jeremy said, "Mother tells me you're an attorney...David."

"Yes, I am."

"She says you're a public defender in New York City."

"Yes."

"But you graduated from Columbia."

"Right again."

Jeremy smiled, but the action looked more like a smirk. "Columbia is a fine school. You must have had offers from a number of firms. Why did you decide to join the public defender's office?"

David shrugged. "I knew I would have the kind of challenges there I wouldn't get in a private law firm."

"Challenges, yes, but hardly compensation," Jeremy said.

David met his gaze. "Believe it or not, there are more important things to me than money."

Bradlee could almost see the wheels turning in Jeremy's head. If David wasn't interested in money, perhaps there was still a chance for *him*. As if to confirm her thoughts, she saw him glance down the table at Iris, who showed no outward reaction whatsoever to David's statement.

"In fact," David said, setting his napkin aside and standing, "maybe this is a good time to set the record straight."

His eyes met Bradlee's for just an instant, then in turn he let his gaze fall on Jeremy, on Edward, then Pamela, and lastly, Iris.

"I didn't come here for your money," David said slowly. "All I want from any of you is the truth."

They all sat silent for a moment, as if what he'd said didn't quite compute. Then Edward, looking as if he needed something other than orange juice this morning, roused himself long enough to murmur, "The truth? What truth?"

"The truth about the night I was kidnapped," David replied. He had everyone's attention now, and Bradlee glanced down the table, observing the various emotions. Jeremy was looking a bit self-satisfied, Edward puzzled, Pamela disgusted, and Iris—

Bradlee couldn't tell what Iris was feeling. It was as if a mask had fallen over the older woman's face, hiding whatever emotions might have been revealed.

"Before my mother died, she told me an incredible story," David continued. "Apparently, Raymond Colter had an accomplice. Someone who was in the house that night. Someone closely connected to this family paid him to kidnap me. That's why I'm here. To find out who stole thirty-two years of my life. And I *will* find out," he finished. "I promise you that."

The silence that followed was deafening. Bradlee could feel the shock permeating the table, and if she hadn't felt so dazed herself, she might have found the Kingsleys' reactions amusing. They weren't used to being blindsided this way.

But as it was, Bradlee was also stunned into silence. Someone who had been in this house that night—perhaps someone at this very table—had paid Raymond Colter to kidnap Adam. Someone *had* been in the nursery that night. Someone *had* stood over Bradlee's bed.

It hadn't been a nightmare. The shadow was real.

Bradlee felt herself trembling all over as she realized the implication of David's words. He was looking for the truth and unless she missed her guess, whoever had been in the nursery that night would do anything to keep him from finding it.

But why should that be so shocking? Wasn't that exactly the reason *she* had come back here?

Presently, everyone at the table seemed to collect their wits. Pamela said in shocked outrage, "How dare you accuse any of us—"

Edward muttered, "My God, how could you think—"

Jeremy pushed back his chair and stood. "Now, see here—"

Only Iris and Bradlee remained silent. Bradlee glanced down at the end of the table. Iris's complexion had gone nearly as white as her hair. She had a hand to her heart, as if near collapse. When David spun away from the table and strode from the room, she put her hand out as if to stop him, but still she said nothing.

Bradlee scraped back her own chair and stood. "If you'll excuse me..." She hurried from the room, feeling all eyes on her as she escaped through the kitchen, in the same direction David had taken.

She followed the flagstone walkway that led to the garages. David was just backing his car out, and Bradlee waved him down. He stopped when he saw her and got out of the car.

She hurried toward him. "Did you mean what you said in there?" she asked breathlessly. "Did your mother really tell you that?"

"I don't expect you to believe me," he said. "I'm

not even sure I believe it. But it's something I have to find out.''

"I do believe you," Bradlee stated quietly.

He'd started to say something else, then stopped. He stared down at her, his eyes darkening with suspicion. "Why?"

The words tumbled out of her, as if in a rush to be heard. "Because I've always thought someone was in the nursery that night. Someone who didn't belong there. I think I may have seen the kidnapper."

He grabbed her arms. "You mean you saw Raymond Colter?"

Bradlee shook her head. "No. It was someone I knew. Someone—"

His grip tightened. "Who was it? Tell me who it was."

"I don't know—"

"But you just said it was someone you knew."

Bradlee winced as his fingers dug into her skin. Almost instantly, his hold on her eased but he didn't release her.

"I think it was someone I knew. But I didn't see a face. All I saw was...a shadow."

Disappointment flashed in his eyes. "Then how do you know it was someone you knew?"

"It's just...a feeling I have." Bradlee realized how lame her words sounded, and she felt like weeping all of a sudden. She wanted to help him. More than anything, she wanted to help him.

"A feeling." Abruptly David released her. All the urgency faded from his expression.

Bradlee ran a hand through her hair. "Ever since the kidnapping, I've had nightmares. There's this shadow standing over my bed, and I know it's someone I know, but I can't see a face. Maybe because I don't want to see it."

His eyes narrowed at that. "You were only three years old back then. The kidnapping must have terrified you. It's only natural you'd have nightmares."

This time, it was she who grabbed his arm. "But I know I saw something that night. I've always known it. It's haunted me for years, thinking that if I could just remember, I might know where you were. I might be able to bring you back."

"Everyone thought I was dead."

"I never did."

"Maybe you should have. Maybe the nightmares would have gone away."

She caught his arm again when he would have turned away. "I want to help you, David. Please. I...owe you that much."

He stared at her hand on his arm, then slowly lifted his gaze to meet hers. His eyes were cool and distant, revealing none of the emotion, none of the warmth she'd glimpsed the night before, outside the nursery.

"You don't owe me anything. And I don't want your help. This is something I have to do on my own."

"But, Adam—"

If possible, his eyes grew even colder. "My name is David. *David.* I'm not that little boy you remember. I'm a grown man, Bradlee. I don't need a guardian angel anymore. And if you know what's good for you, you'll keep your mouth shut. You won't tell anyone what you just told me.''

''I don't understand.''

''It's pretty damned simple. If someone in this house—someone connected to this family—had something to do with my kidnapping, what do you think they'd do if they thought you saw something that night?''

A shiver of fear swept over Bradlee. ''But you just told the family that you're going to find out the truth. Whoever is responsible for your kidnapping is bound to find out what you plan to do. You've deliberately put your own life in danger.''

He got into the car and slammed the door. ''Go back to L.A., Bradlee. Back to your photography. Let me handle this.''

''You still don't get it, do you?'' She put her hands on the open window of the car and stared down at him. ''I'm not going anywhere. Not until I know you're safe.''

''Just what I need,'' he muttered. He gave her an exasperated glance. ''All right, get in. I have a feeling you'd be more dangerous going off half-cocked somewhere on your own than staying with me. At least this way I can keep an eye on you.''

''Where are we going?'' Bradlee gave him a dazzling smile. He blinked twice before he answered her.

''Just get in. I need to get away from here for a

while. When I know where we're going, I'll let you know.''

Bradlee, feeling unaccountably elated, hurried around to the other side of the car before he could change his mind. But as she opened the door, she glanced up and her elation faded. A movement at one of the second-floor windows drew her gaze, and Bradlee shivered, certain that someone was standing up there, watching them.

Someone who was not very pleased to see the two of them together.

BRADLEE AND DAVID were silent as they drove into Memphis. To her surprise, he seemed to know the city fairly well, and as they headed down Poplar Avenue, toward the entrance to Overton Park, Bradlee asked him why he'd driven his car all the way from New York rather than flying.

"I like to have my own transportation," he replied. "I don't like relying on others."

"So I noticed. But you could have rented a car."

He patted the leather seat affectionately. "Not one like this."

"She is a beauty," Bradlee agreed, although quite frankly, she preferred the Porsche—both the rental and the one she had back home.

He pulled into the park and found a spot near the tennis courts. They got out to walk. "How did you know about the park?" Bradlee asked. "You haven't been to Memphis before, have you?"

"Not in a while," he said dryly, then shrugged.

"Actually, I studied a map before I came. I like to cover all my bases."

All your escape routes, you mean, Bradlee thought, shivering in the warm morning sunshine. "Tell me about your life in New York," she said, as they found an empty bench and sat down. It was a weekday, so the park was almost empty. A mother pushing a baby stroller walked by, and David waited until she was gone before he answered.

"It's a good life," he said simply. "I know what all of you must think of my—of the woman who raised me, but in some ways—in most, really—she was a good person."

"I can believe that," Bradlee said softly. "Seeing the man you've turned out to be."

He stared down at her for a moment, then shifted his gaze, staring off into the distance. "You don't know anything about me."

"I know you graduated with top honors from Columbia University. I know you chose to join the public defender's office instead of some elitist law firm. You obviously care more about the law than you do about money, and that tells me a lot." Probably more than he realized.

"I'm not as altruistic as you may think," he said grimly. "Until very recently, I was considering joining one of those elitist law firms. The elitist of the elite."

"But you didn't."

"No, but I could still change my mind. Don't see me for the person you knew at the age of three, Bradlee. A lot's happened to me since then. To you, too, I would imagine.''

''We grew up,'' she said. ''You in New York and me in California. A whole continent apart, and yet here we are.''

As if not wanting to explore the connection, he asked, ''So what's life like in L.A.?''

''Oh, you know. Swimming pools. Movie stars.'' He smiled at that, and Bradlee thought, *What a nice smile he has. What an attractive man he is.* And at that moment, she didn't think of him as Adam at all, but as David Powers, a very intriguing attorney.

''Actually, it's taken me a long time to build a career in fashion photography out there. The competition is almost as fierce as in New York.''

''You seem to be doing all right for yourself.'' His gaze studied her for a moment, and Bradlee knew that he was assessing her success by the way she looked, by the way she dressed. Her clothes were simple—jeans and a cotton shirt—but they were expensive, carrying exclusive labels that Bradlee had always taken for granted. She didn't think David did.

She shrugged. ''I guess so.''

''Anyone special in your life?''

''Not really.''

''Why not?''

Her gaze lifted and met his. ''I guess I just haven't met the right person. So here I sit with my biological clock slowly ticking away.''

''It's not too late,'' David said. ''You've got plenty of time.''

"Not if I want a houseful of kids." She reached down to pluck a blade of grass and run it through her fingers.

He lifted a dark brow in amusement. "A whole houseful? One or two wouldn't do?"

"For starters, I guess." She tickled her chin with the grass. David found the motion soothing. Mesmerizing. He'd never known anyone like Bradlee. She was quiet and restful, and yet he knew there was passion simmering beneath the placid surface. He'd had a glimpse of it last night, when he'd wanted to kiss her and her eyes had told him, *Yes, go ahead. But be prepared for the consequences.*

David suspected the consequences of becoming involved with a woman like Bradlee Fitzgerald were far greater than he could imagine. Maybe it was a good thing he was engaged.

"I was an only child," she was saying. "And I always told myself that I would give my children lots of brothers and sisters to play with. They would never be lonely like I was."

"I was an only child, too," he said. "Or at least, I thought I was."

Bradlee's smile turned wistful. "I'm sorry you never got to meet Andrew. They say there's a very special bond between twins."

"That's what they say," David agreed. But he'd never felt it. He didn't feel anything for his dead brother except a passing regret that the two of them would never know each other.

Bradlee tossed the blade of grass away and

glanced up at him. "So. We've talked about everything except what's really on our minds."

He stared at a couple heading toward the tennis courts.

"What are we going to do about finding out who paid Raymond Colter to kidnap you?" she persisted.

"*We* aren't going to do anything," he replied. "I don't want you involved in this, Bradlee."

"But I am involved. I may be the one person who can help you find the truth. And I think I know where we can start."

David swore under his breath. She might not be like any woman he'd ever known, but she had one trait in common with *every* woman he'd ever known: She was stubborn as hell.

"I'm almost afraid to ask what you have in mind."

Her impish grin made her seem hardly more than a teenager. David suddenly wondered what it would have been like if the two of them had grown up together. Would they have remained close friends? A line from an Ernest Hemingway novel popped into his head: *"It was pretty to think so."*

"I want to be hypnotized," she said.

"Were you ever hypnotized before? Back then, I mean?"

Bradlee shook her head. "The psychiatrist my parents took me to thought I was too young. And as I grew older, I suppose I just didn't think about it that much—only when I had the nightmares. I guess in a way, I was afraid to remember."

"What about now?"

She shrugged. "I'm older, wiser, tougher. I can handle it."

But in spite of her outward calm, David saw a glimmer of fear in her eyes, and he wondered if she knew what she was getting herself into.

Did he?

"WE'RE IN LUCK," Bradlee said, hanging up David's cell phone. She gave him a broad smile, a smile that was far more confident than the way she actually felt inside. A tremor of fear started in her stomach and worked its way outward, until she was trembling all over. What had she gotten herself into?

The notion of being hypnotized, of unveiling her innermost thoughts and fears to a perfect stranger, was terrifying. But it was too late to back out now.

She smiled again, willing her courage. "Dr. Scott remembers me. She was fairly young when my parents took me to see her after the kidnapping, but she's semiretired now. Only works part-time. Anyway, she's agreed to see me this afternoon."

"Are you sure you want to do this?" The intensity of his gaze made Bradlee even more nervous. She turned to stare out the window of his car.

"I'm sure. It's the only way I'll ever know if that shadow really has a face. If I really saw someone in the nursery that night, or if it was just a nightmare."

"All right, where to?" David asked, starting the engine and backing out of the parking space.

"Her office is downtown, on Union. Get us out of the park and I'll give you directions from there."

BRADLEE DIDN'T REMEMBER Dr. Scott—only her name. And even if she had remembered her, she doubted she would have recognized her. People changed considerably in thirty-two years. In Dr. Scott's case, she'd been only a few years out of medical school back then, and now she was nearing sixty, gray-haired, stoop-shouldered, but had blue eyes that still gleamed with intelligence.

She ushered Bradlee and David into her inner office and motioned for them to sit. "I got out your file after you called, but I remember your case well," she said, taking a seat behind her desk. "Primarily because of the notoriety of the kidnapping. I read in the paper that a private detective has located Adam Kingsley. Imagine that, after all this time."

Bradlee exchanged a glance with David. They'd agreed ahead of time not to reveal his identity. "That's why I'm here," she said. "I've always had a feeling there was something about that night that's remained hidden in my subconscious. I've had nightmares about it all these years." Bradlee leaned forward in her chair, her tone urgent. "Dr. Scott, I want you to hypnotize me."

"So you said on the phone." Dr. Scott gazed at Bradlee thoughtfully. "Do you know much about hypnosis?"

Bradlee shrugged. "Only that you go into a trance,

and it's possible to remember things from your past. Things you've buried.''

"It's not quite that simple. Hypnosis is not without risk. Anytime you go looking for memories, you may recover more than you bargain for. You have to be prepared to deal with everything that surfaces.''

"I am. This is very important to me, Dr. Scott. Vitally important.''

Dr. Scott studied her for a moment, then nodded. "All right, then. Let's get started." She turned to David, "If you would just wait for us outside—''

"No, I want him to stay," Bradlee said. She glanced at David. "He needs to stay.''

Dr. Scott shrugged. "If that's what you want, I have no objection." She motioned for Bradlee to lie down on the sofa, then pulled up a chair facing her. She explained that hypnosis was a form of deep relaxation, and that no one could be made to do anything while "under" that he or she would not normally be willing to do.

David watched the whole process in fascination. Bradlee's whole body grew lax, her eyes closed, her breathing evened.

"Bradlee, if you can hear me, nod your head," Dr. Scott instructed.

Her head moved up and down almost imperceptibly.

"Can you talk to me?''

"Yes." It was barely a whisper.

"You're very relaxed and so if you have a difficult time speaking, just nod or shake your head. Okay?''

A nod.

They began with more recent events and questions Bradlee had no difficulty responding to. Gradually, however, Dr. Scott took her back to the year of the kidnapping.

"You're three years old, Bradlee. What are you doing at this moment?"

Bradlee smiled. "My birthday. Having a party."

David watched the transformation in astonishment. Her face had grown even more relaxed and the years seemed to melt away. There was an innocent quality to her smile, a softness in her voice that could have belonged to a child.

"Who's at your party, Bradlee?"

"Friends."

"What friends?"

"Ellen."

"Who else?"

"Debbie. Andrew. Adam."

"Who is Adam?"

"Friend. Best friend."

"All right, Bradlee, let's leave the party and skip ahead a bit. It's the night of June 24th. Do you know where you are?"

Bradlee's brows drew together in concentration. "Car."

"You're in a car?"

She nodded.

"Who's with you in the car?"

"Mommy. Daddy." A long pause, then, "Angry."

"Your parents are angry with you?"

She shook her head.

"Are they angry with each other?"

A nod. "Scared."

"Their arguing frightens you? Are their voices raised?"

A nod.

"Can you hear what they're saying?"

Another pause. She frowned in confusion.

"What are your parents arguing about, Bradlee?"

"Money." When she spoke again, her voice was deeper than a child's. "Dammit, Mary, I told you I have everything under control."

"It's okay, Bradlee. You're relaxed. Very, very relaxed. Nothing can hurt you. Do you understand?"

Bradlee nodded and murmured something David couldn't understand.

"You're at the Kingsley mansion, Bradlee, in the nursery with Adam and Andrew. Can you see them?"

She nodded and smiled. "Funny. Andrew's funny." Her voice was childlike again.

"What about Adam?"

Her smiled faded. "Sad. Crying."

"Adam's crying?"

She nodded.

"Do you know why?"

She flinched. "Hit him."

"Someone hit him?"

Her breathing deepened. She couldn't seem to answer.

Dr. Scott said, "Just nod or shake your head, Bradlee."

She nodded.

"Who hit Adam, Bradlee?"

"Mother."

"*His* mother?"

When she nodded again, David leaned toward Dr. Scott and whispered, "Ask her if it was Adam's stepmother?"

"Bradlee, was the person who hit Adam his stepmother?"

She nodded.

"Did you see her hit him?"

"Andrew saw."

"Did anyone come into the nursery while you were there that night, Bradlee?"

A pause. Then, "Adam's daddy. His mother. Night, night."

"They came in to say good-night?"

She nodded.

"Who else?"

"My mommy."

"Not your daddy?"

Silence.

"Did anyone else come into the nursery that night?"

"Adam's grandmother. Jenny. All night, night."

"Okay, Bradlee, everyone has come in to say good-night. You and Andrew and Adam are all in bed now. Can you see what's happening?"

"Dark."

"It's dark in the room?"

"Can't...sleep."

"Why not?"

"Adam..."

"Is Adam still crying?"

"Sleeping..."

"Then why can't you sleep?"

Silence. Her eyelids fluttered rapidly. "Save... him."

"Save him from what?"

"*Save* him," she said stubbornly.

"You have to save Adam?"

She nodded vigorously.

"From what? Adam isn't in any danger right at this moment, is he?"

Bradlee fretted. "Mother hit him."

"You're afraid his stepmother will come in and hit him again?"

She nodded.

"All right, so the twins are sleeping, and you remain awake to watch over Adam. Is anyone else in the room, Bradlee?"

She started to shake her head, then gasped.

"What is it, Bradlee?"

"Shadow..." The word was barely a whisper. "Shadow...by Adam."

"Someone is standing by Adam's bed?"

She nodded. Her facial expression became tense. "Touching him."

"The shadow is touching Adam?"

"His...face." She paused. "Can't...breathe."

David exchanged a glance with Dr. Scott. A chill slid along his spine.

"Who can't breathe, Bradlee? You?"

"Adam…" She wrinkled her nose. "Smell…"

"What do you smell?" When she didn't respond, Dr. Scott prompted again, "What do you smell, Bradlee?"

"Don't know. Don't like it."

"Is the shadow still standing by Adam's bed?"

A pause. "Gone."

"Gone where?"

Another look of confusion. Sweat beaded on Bradlee's brow. "Window open…waving."

Dr. Scott glanced at David. He felt his own pulse quicken as he leaned toward her. "Ask her if the shadow opened the balcony window."

"Bradlee, are you saying someone—the shadow—has opened the balcony window?"

"Waving," she whispered.

"The shadow is waving to someone?"

A nod. Then another gasp. "No!"

"What is the shadow doing now, Bradlee?"

"Coming…back…" She squeezed her eyes shut, her words a terrified whisper. "Sleep, Bradlee. Sleep."

"It's all right, Bradlee. Whatever you see is okay. The shadow can't hurt you. Can't touch you. Do you understand?"

A nod.

"Is the shadow coming back into the room? Is it coming toward you?"

Bradlee drew in a sharp breath. "I…know."

"What do you know?"

"I *know*."

"You know who the shadow is?"

Silence.

"Who is it, Bradlee?"

"Can't."

"You can't see who it is?"

"Can't tell." The sweat was rolling off her face now. Bradlee flinched. "Hurt me. Hurt me."

"You're afraid the shadow will hurt you?"

"Don't tell. Mustn't tell. Hurt me."

David couldn't tear his gaze from Bradlee. It was like glimpsing the way she must have been that night, innocent and vulnerable and very frightened. And yet she'd stayed awake to protect him.

"You're safe, Bradlee," Dr. Scott reminded her. "The shadow can't touch you."

Bradlee's hands flew out in front of her. Her head thrashed from side to side. "No!"

"What is it, Bradlee? What's happening?"

"Hurt me! Hurt Adam!"

"The shadow is hurting you?"

"Can't breathe!"

"Bradlee, answer me. What's happening?"

"Can't breathe!"

"Bradlee—"

"Can't breathe!"

Chapter Five

Bradlee awoke feeling refreshed. She tried to stifle a yawn. "What happened?"

"Don't you remember?" David glanced at Dr. Scott. "You said she'd remember."

"Give her time," Dr. Scott advised.

Bradlee stretched. "I do remember some of it. It's all sort of hazy, but it's coming back in flashes." She sat up excitedly. "I think we're close to a breakthrough. Can we try again? Maybe I'll remember something else."

"You've had enough for one day," Dr. Scott said. She got up and walked back to her desk. "Let me caution you about something, Bradlee. We're treading on fragile ground here. Age-regression hypnosis can be very tricky, and the power of suggestion can't be discounted. Patients have been known to create false memories, even in the deepest of trances, because of things they've heard or seen, or maybe even intuited."

Bradlee looked at her in surprise. "Are you saying that's what you think I did?"

"Not necessarily. But the notoriety of the kidnapping concerns me a bit. It's been in and out of the news for years. You're bound to have heard things about that night, various theories as to how and why Adam Kingsley was kidnapped. It's always been speculated that more than one person was involved."

"That's true," Bradlee agreed. "But I've had this recurring nightmare for years, ever since the kidnapping. That's why my parents first brought me to see you."

"Yes, and I thought at the time the shadow you told me about was probably a manifestation of your own fear of being kidnapped. That's why you felt so threatened by it."

"And now?"

"Now, I'm not sure what to think. Something obviously terrified you that night. Whether it was the kidnapping itself or something else, you've never gotten over it. I don't think those nightmares will go away until you find out once and for all what that shadow represents to you."

"And if it does represent someone I saw in the nursery that night?"

Dr. Scott glanced up. "Then I think you have to be very, very careful."

DAVID WAS SILENT on the drive home. Bradlee couldn't tell if he was in deep thought or a very bad mood. Judging by the way he glowered at the road, she suspected it was the latter.

Finally, when they'd left the city behind and had

turned onto the two-lane road that would take them to the mansion, Bradlee asked, "Are you upset with me?"

He shrugged. "Why would I be upset with you?"

"Because I couldn't remember everything."

"That wasn't your fault."

"I know, but..." She paused, biting her lip. "You seem angry or in a bad mood or something. What's wrong?"

"Nothing's wrong. I just don't feel like talking."

"David—"

He swore under his breath. "Are you always like this?"

"Like what?" she asked defensively.

"So...relentless." He swore again, training his eyes on the road.

Hurt, Bradlee turned to stare out her window.

Beside her, David muttered something under his breath. Then he swung the car off the road and parked. They sat in silence for a moment, then he finally said, "Look, I'm sorry. I shouldn't take my bad mood out on you."

She sniffed. "I was just trying to help."

"I know, it's just... *Damn.*" He hit the steering wheel with his fist. "I didn't think this was going to be so hard."

Abruptly he got out of the car and slammed the door. At the risk of being thought relentless again, Bradlee got out, too. She walked around to stand beside him, but she didn't say a word, just stared off into the distance, waiting.

"It shouldn't matter," he finally said.

"What shouldn't?"

His expression hardened. "It was all a long time ago. I've got a good life. Why should it matter?"

"How could it *not* matter?"

He didn't seem to hear her. His eyes looked distant, bleak. "Seeing you in there like that made me realize how it must have been. What they did to me. To us. We were just little kids."

"I know." Bradlee shivered.

"I think I've remembered something," he said, frowning. "I had sort of a flash while you were under. I think I remember being in a car with a stranger—Colter, I guess—and begging to go home. He told me he was taking me to see my mother. I knew my mother was dead, but I kept hoping he was telling me the truth. But when I saw the woman he was talking about, I knew she wasn't my mother. Not at first. Then I guess I started to believe that she was. What choice did I have?" His tone grew bitter. "I couldn't go back home."

"I can't imagine how it must have been for you," Bradlee said.

"She lied to me about everything, even told me my father was a war hero. My whole life has been a lie. I don't know who to believe anymore. Who I can trust."

Not caring this time if she was being relentless or not, Bradlee placed her hand on his arm. "There's me," she said softly. "You can trust me. I've always been here—you just didn't know it."

He looked down at her then, his eyes dark and

intense, stormy with emotion. Bradlee trembled as he lifted his hand to cup the back of her neck and draw her to him. He cradled her head against his shoulder as she slipped her arms around his waist.

For the longest time, they stood there on the side of the road, holding each other, and Bradlee thought in wonder that it was she who had been lost for all that time—lost and alone. But after thirty-two years, she'd finally found her way back home.

THAT NIGHT, DAVID placed a call to Rachel. He'd just gotten out of the shower and was lying on the bed, feet crossed at the ankles, head propped against his pillows. He caught her on her way out, and she didn't try to hide her annoyance.

"David, where are you?"

He hesitated, not ready to tell her where he was, or even *who* he was. He wasn't sure why. When the Kingsleys made their announcement, everyone would know. His name and picture would likely be run in every major newspaper in the country. He knew he couldn't keep his identity a secret much longer, but for now, he wanted to enjoy what little anonymity he had left.

"Daddy is still furious with you, you know," Rachel was saying. "You know how he harbors a grudge. It was bad enough that you canceled your appointment with him like that, but to call and announce to him you weren't interested in joining the firm. To not even pay him the courtesy of telling him in person."

David rolled his eyes. He'd heard this all before.

Rachel's father wasn't the only one who held a grudge. "I'll apologize when I see him. Something unexpected came up. I had to get away for a few days."

She paused. Then, with uncharacteristic uncertainty, she asked, "Is it us?"

"No." At least, it hadn't been when he left New York.

"Be honest with me, David. Is there someone else?"

A pair of soft brown eyes materialized in his mind. *"I've always been here. You just didn't know it."*

"There's no one else," he said wearily. "I just have a lot going on in my life right now."

"But I'm your fiancée," she said in a wounded tone. "Why can't you tell me what's wrong? Maybe I can help."

When he didn't say anything, she sighed. "I went by your apartment the other day. The super let me in. I told him I was worried about you. I *am* worried about you." She paused again. "There were newspaper clippings all over the place, articles about an old kidnapping. Does that have something to do with why you left town so suddenly? Are you working on a case?"

"In a way," he said evasively.

"I know you're in Memphis."

Alarmed, he sat up in bed. "How the hell do you know that?"

"Your secretary told me she'd made airline reservations for you, which you then had her cancel.

You decided to drive instead. She didn't know where you were staying, though."

He shouldn't have been surprised. With the impressive facilities of Hollingsworth, Beckman and Carr at her disposal, Rachel Hollingsworth could accomplish just about anything. She probably hadn't even missed lunch finding out where he'd gone. The question now was, how could he keep her from coming down here.

"Look, I don't want you to worry about me," he said. "I'm fine. I'm just going through some sort of midlife crisis or something."

"David, you're only thirty-five years old."

"You know I always like to get a head start." When she didn't respond to his lame joke, he said, "Believe me, there's nothing for you to worry about. I'll call you again in a few days."

"When?"

He searched the ceiling. "Saturday. Six o'clock."

"All right, but if you don't get me at home, try my cell phone."

He almost laughed out loud at that. It was a more telling remark about their relationship than she realized. She wouldn't exactly be sitting around waiting for his call, come Saturday. She had things to do, people to see.

"I have to go," he said.

"All right, but—"

"I'll talk to you on Saturday." He hung up before she could respond, and with the connection severed, his life in New York—and Rachel Hollingsworth—instantly seemed a million miles away.

Chapter Six

The next day, Bradlee met her father for lunch at Pier 21, a seafood restaurant overlooking the Mississippi River. While he painstakingly cross-examined the waitress on the specials, Bradlee watched a tugboat pull a barge slowly upstream.

"Now, make sure you keep those drinks coming," he instructed, handing the now harried waitress his menu. When she left, he smiled across the table at Bradlee. "So tell me, darlin'. To what do I owe this unexpected pleasure? I got the feeling the other night you weren't exactly happy with your old man."

"Why would I be unhappy with you?"

He tried to look contrite but couldn't quite manage it. "I know you don't approve of Crystal."

"It's not up to me to approve or disapprove of your marriages. I assume you know what you're doing."

He folded his arms on the table and leaned toward her. "Darlin', it may surprise you to know that I've never loved anyone the way I loved your mother. I don't think I ever will."

Bradlee's gaze was openly skeptical. "Then why did you divorce her?"

He sighed, running a hand through his thinning, but still-dark hair. "We had different philosophies on life, your mother and me. I was ambitious. I wanted to be somebody. Your mother couldn't understand that."

Or was it because she put her daughter's needs before her own? Bradlee thought. *Unlike you.*

Aloud she said, "I thought you divorced her because she moved to Los Angeles."

He eyed her sadly. "That was part of it. The last straw, I guess you might say. Our problems started long before that, though."

"You two used to fight about money, didn't you?" Bradlee said. "I would hear you."

"That's impossible. You were just a baby."

"No, I do remember. You were fighting about money the night Adam Kingsley was kidnapped."

He frowned. "What's that got to do with anything?"

"Nothing. I just remembered, that's all."

Her father sighed wearily. "Your mother never thought money, or material things, were important because she'd never wanted for anything. She came from money, and money *isn't* important if you've always had it. I grew up differently. Your Uncle Harper and I had to fight and scratch for everything we got, but we were both determined to claw our way out of the poorhouse and make something of ourselves. When your mother left, I'd just been hired by one of the biggest law firms in Memphis, and Harper was Edward Kingsley's campaign manager. We were connected, Bradlee. In solid with the movers and shakers in this town. Against all odds, my brother and I had made it, and then suddenly, out of the blue, your mother wanted me to just give it all up. Start all over out there in California.''

It had hardly come out of the blue, but Bradlee decided not to quibble. ''I'd forgotten that Harper was Edward Kingsley's campaign manager,'' she murmured, though she hadn't really. Harper Fitzgerald had managed many successful political campaigns, both state and national. In fact, Bradlee didn't think he'd ever lost one. That was why his services were still so heavily in demand even at his age.

Her father leaned toward her. ''Harper was brilliant back then. We both were, if I do say so myself. We knew how to handle ourselves, how to turn almost any situation to our advantage. But to pull Kingsley's campaign out of the toilet like that, to get him elected after all the negative publicity following his wife's death and his untimely second marriage to Pamela...I didn't think he could do it. No one did. I thought he'd go down with a sinking ship.''

The waitress brought their orders, and after she'd placed his plate in front of him, Bradlee's father picked up his empty glass and rattled the ice cubes. The waitress hurried off to bring him a fresh drink.

Bradlee stared down at her own plate. The grilled shrimp smelled delicious, but she wasn't hungry.

Toying with her rice, she watched her father attack his food with gusto.

"How did Harper manage to save Edward's campaign?" she finally asked, when her father made no attempt to pursue their previous conversation.

He speared a shrimp, savored it, then glanced up. "It was a fluke, really, but Harper had the foresight to see it when the rest of us didn't. He called it the sympathy factor. The kidnapping swayed public opinion in Edward's favor, and Harper played it for all it was worth."

"That seems a little cold-blooded." Bradlee pushed her plate aside, untouched.

Her father gestured with his fork. "Politics is a cold-blooded sport, Bradlee, not for the faint of heart. Besides, it wasn't as if Harper kidnapped the boy or anything. He saw an opportunity and seized it, and something good came out of a tragedy. What's wrong with that?"

Bradlee didn't bother to explain. What was the point? She and her father operated on different wavelengths. They always had. She suddenly had new sympathy for her mother.

"You and Harper were both at the fund-raiser the night Adam was kidnapped, weren't you?"

Her father polished off his second drink. "Along with a lot of other people. Anyone who was anyone."

"Like who?"

He shrugged, glancing around for the waitress. "All the Kingsleys, of course. The mayor. A senator, a couple of congressmen, all the party leaders. Even Cotton Weathers made an appearance, although we never could figure out how that son of a bitch got past the guards. He sure as hell didn't have an invitation.''

"Who was Cotton Weathers?"

Her father spotted the waitress and beckoned her over. "What's your name, honey?"

She glanced at Bradlee, who could do little more than give her a sympathetic smile. "Amber."

"Amber." He held up his empty glass. "Do you know what this is?"

"Yes, sir. I'm sorry, sir—"

"I thought I made myself clear. There's not much that annoys me worse than having an empty glass sitting in front of me."

The woman's face flushed a bright red. Bradlee said, "Come on, Dad."

He ignored her. "Now I suggest you run along and bring me another drink. And when you see the glass about halfway empty, start making plans to fetch me another. *Capisce?*"

Amber looked as if she couldn't decide whether to burst into tears or dump the remainder of his lunch on his head. Bradlee was rooting for the latter. But instead, Amber managed to smile sweetly and this time, it was she who shot Bradlee a sympathetic glance. "I'll be right back with your drink, sir."

"Dad, for God's sake," Bradlee said in exasperation. "Did you have to make a federal case out of it?"

Her father's eyes narrowed on her. "How many times have I told you, Bradlee, you have to know how to treat these people. They'll walk all over you if you let them."

The waitress brought his drink, paused only long enough to ask if they needed anything else, then hurried away. Bradlee couldn't blame her. She wished she could leave, too.

"Now then," her father said, resuming his meal as though nothing had happened. "Where were we?"

"You were telling me about Cotton Weathers."

"Right. He was the lieutenant governor back then, and he fully expected to be governor when Conners retired. That is, until Edward announced his intention. Cotton hated Edward. There was bad blood between him and all the Kingsleys. Never knew why exactly, except that it went back generations. Cotton swore that night he would do anything to stop Edward from becoming governor. He gloated that he'd been the one to leak the story to the tabloids about Edward's affair with Pamela while his wife was on her deathbed. That very nearly did Edward in. Then Adam was kidnapped and everything changed."

Bradlee studied her napkin for a moment. "You say Cotton hated Edward Kingsley. Do you think he might have had something to do with Adam's kidnapping? Maybe he thought Edward would pull out of the race if one of his sons was kidnapped."

"I don't think even Cotton was that dumb. Besides, Raymond Colter kidnapped Adam. The man admitted it. He's serving a life sentence in prison."

"I know that," Bradlee said. "But he might have had an accomplice."

Her father stared at her accusingly, pointing at her with his fork. "I know where all this is coming from. I heard about the accusations David Powers made at breakfast yesterday morning."

Bradlee looked up in surprise. "From who?"

He shrugged. "From Jeremy Willows."

She should have known. Jeremy Willows was a partner in her father's law firm.

"I didn't think you two were on speaking terms," she said. "Not after Iris gave you the Kingsley account instead of him."

Her father grinned—a charming, boyish grin that made him seem far younger than his sixty-plus years. "He sulked around the office for a few days, but he got over it. Besides, he knows I'll be retiring in another few years. He'd be a fool to leave the firm now."

"What all did he tell you?" Bradlee asked, not wanting to stray too far from the subject.

"Just what I said, that Powers accused someone connected to the family of having orchestrated his kidnapping. Which is ridiculous. That woman who disappeared with him—what was her name?—she obviously had a screw loose somewhere. How could anyone believe anything she said?"

"I used to think I saw someone come into the nursery that night," Bradlee reminded him.

"That was nothing more than a nightmare. Your

mother didn't help matters by carting you off to that psychiatrist. If you ask me, she made things worse.''

"I'm not so sure it was just a nightmare," Bradlee said.

Her father pushed his plate aside and stared at her. "I don't know what it was about that boy, but you always did have some kind of fixation about him. Like you had to take care of him or something. That's what you're doing now, darlin', and if you don't mind my saying so, I'm not sure it's all that healthy.''

"I'm just trying to help him," Bradlee defended. "Why is that so difficult for you to understand?''

He leaned toward her, lowering his voice. "I understand this. The moment Iris Kingsley dies, Adam Kingsley will be one of the wealthiest men in this country. A man with that kind of money is bound to have enemies. If you ask me, what happened to him in the past is the least of his worries now.''

WHILE BRADLEE WAS having lunch with her father, David had already made the drive up to the state penitentiary. As he sat in the visitors' room behind a bulletproof screen, he had no idea whether Raymond Colter would agree to talk to him or not. He'd almost convinced himself this was a bad idea to begin with when the door on the other side of the screen opened, and a guard led one of the prisoners through.

In his mind, David had created an image of Raymond Colter from his mother's description. He'd pictured a cop, mid-thirties, tall, muscular, good-looking. What he hadn't taken into account were the thirty-two intervening years. Raymond Colter was an old man now, thin and wiry, with grizzled hair and faded eyes. Those eyes narrowed on David as he shuffled over and sat in the chair behind the Plexiglas.

For a long moment, neither of them said anything, just sat staring at each other. David wasn't sure what it was he felt. This man had taken him from his home, kept him from his family, let the world think he was dead.

I should hate you, he thought. I should despise you for what you did to me.

But for some reason he didn't. For some reason, David didn't feel much of anything.

Raymond Colter leaned toward the speaker in the Plexiglas. "So you're the Kingsley boy, eh? I wouldn't have recognized you. You've changed." He grinned, and suddenly the emotions that had eluded David earlier came rushing over him. Anger, like he had never known before, shot through him, and he knew exactly why the bulletproof shield was necessary—not always for the protection of the visitor, but in some cases, in *this* case, for the prisoner's well-being.

He leaned toward the speaker. "You're lucky you're in prison, old man."

Something shifted in Colter's eyes. Remorse? David doubted it. "I'm spending the rest of my life behind bars, and my only son is dead. Don't tell me I'm lucky, boy.''

David had read about Colter's son, how he had somehow learned his father was guilty of the kidnapping and had died trying to keep the truth from coming out. Trying to keep an innocent man in prison. At that moment, David couldn't feel much sympathy for father *or* son.

''Besides,'' Colter said, studying him through the glass screen. ''What are you complaining about? Looks like Sally did all right by you.''

''Sally?''

''I guess you know her by another name. The woman who took off with you. How is she?''

''She's dead,'' David told him. ''But I didn't come here to make small talk with you. I want to ask you a question, and you damn well better give me a straight answer. You owe me that much.''

Colter gave a short bark of a laugh. ''I'm paying my debt. Right here in this stinking hellhole. I don't owe you anything.''

''Who helped you?'' David asked, watching Colter's face, noticing the tic at the corner of his left eye. ''Who paid you to kidnap me?''

Colter laughed. ''No one paid me to do anything. I came up with the idea all by my lonesome. I nabbed you from the nursery and had the ransom money all to myself.''

He was lying. David had defended too many sleazes like Colter not to recognize it. It was clients like him who sometimes made sleep hard to come by. "The security at the mansion was tight that night—an alarm system, guards patrolling the grounds. The whole bit. There was no way you could have pulled it off alone."

"You're forgetting something." Colter sat back in his chair and smiled. "The guards were all off-duty police officers. I worked there myself every chance I got. I knew that place like the back of my hand. I knew the alarm would be turned off that night because of all the guests. I knew exactly when and where the guards would patrol. It was a simple matter to hide on the grounds and wait for the light in the nursery to go out. Then all I had to do was scale the wall to the balcony, carry the boy out of the nursery, and lower him to the ground with a rope." He seemed to have forgotten that David was that boy.

"Without making a sound?" he asked in disbelief. "Without waking me up?"

Colter shrugged. "Lots of ways to silence a kid."

"Drugs?"

Colter shrugged again without answering, and David remembered something Bradlee had said under hypnosis. That the shadow had been standing beside his bed, touching his face. Could someone have used drugs—ether, maybe—on him to make sure he didn't wake up when Colter came into the room? Would that explain the smell Bradlee hadn't liked?

"All right, supposing you could have avoided the guards," David said, "and somehow managed to scale the wall to the balcony without being seen. What about the French doors? The nanny swore she'd locked them before she went to bed. And the police found no sign of a forced entry."

Colter, still smiling, said, "The police figured the nanny was either mistaken or lying because she forgot to lock up before going to bed."

"Yes, but the problem with that theory is that *you* were the police back then. You made damned sure you got yourself assigned to the investigation. How much evidence did you destroy to cover your own tracks? Or someone else's?"

Raymond Colter's dark eyes took his measure. "You're a smart guy, Kingsley. I can tell you've given this a lot of thought. But it was all a long time ago. It's water under the bridge, as they say. Even if I answered your questions, what's it going to change? You'll still be Adam Kingsley and I'll still be locked away in this rat hole. Take my advice, boy. The past is best forgotten."

"Yes, but I don't seem to be able to forget," David said grimly.

Colter shrugged. "Well, maybe you'd better find a way to do just that. Maybe you'd best get on with your life and forget all about your little conspiracy theories."

"It's more than a theory and you know it," David accused. "What I can't figure out is why you're still trying to protect your accomplice. From where I'm sitting, you don't have much to lose by talking."

Colter glanced around, then leaned forward. "Granted, this isn't much of a life, but we all cling to what we've got left, don't we?"

"Are you saying you're afraid to talk?"

Colter's features hardened. His eyes grew cold, deadly—the look of a man who'd learned the hard way how to survive. "You're Adam Kingsley, boy. You're one rich son of a bitch, now. People are going to be gunning for you just because of who you are and what you've got. If I were you, I wouldn't go looking for trouble."

He stood and the guard came over to take him back to his cell. At the door, Colter paused and turned back to say something. He wasn't near the speaker now so David couldn't hear the words. But he thought what Raymond Colter said was, "Watch your back, boy."

David stood and headed for the door on his side of the partition. He suddenly couldn't wait to get outside into the sunshine.

Chapter Seven

By the end of the week, the awkwardness in the Kingsley household was beginning to tell on everyone. Jeremy stayed away as much as possible, Edward had taken to drinking again, and Pamela grew even colder and angrier. Only Iris seemed to thrive under the pressure. She became stronger every day until she was both physically and mentally back to normal.

On Friday night, she announced at dinner that she planned to have a party to introduce David to their close friends and business associates.

"The news is bound to get out sooner or later," she said. "It's already common knowledge that you've been found, but they don't yet know you've come back home. If we make the announcement ourselves, we can invite only those reporters who we know won't try to sensationalize the story."

"I hardly think a party is appropriate," Jeremy muttered. "Considering he thinks we're all a pack of criminals." He glowered across the table at David.

"Not at all," David said smoothly. "I believe

Raymond Colter had only one accomplice, and since you were eight years old at the time, you're the one person here who's pretty much in the clear.''

Jeremy started to retort, but Iris stopped him with a look. "I'll hear no more about it," she said. "It's ridiculous to think that anyone in this house or anyone connected to this family might have conspired to kidnap one of my grandsons." Her gaze hardened as she glanced around the table. "They would not have dared."

"A party might be a good idea," Edward murmured, studying his drink. "God knows, there hasn't been anything in this house worth celebrating in years."

"And whose fault is that?" Pamela demanded. She addressed her question to Edward, but her gaze slid to Iris.

"I remember when Edward and Carolyn were married," Iris reminisced, her words uncharacteristically wistful. "The ceremony was beautiful and the reception magnificent. It was a celebration in the Kingsley tradition. And then, of course, when the twins were born, we had even more cause to rejoice...." Her words trailed off, her expression spiteful as she glanced at her daughter-in-law. "Since then, however, one disaster after another has befallen this family."

Her point couldn't have been clearer. She was including Pamela's marriage to Edward in those disasters. It took a moment to sink in for Pamela, and then she pushed back her chair and stood. Throwing down her napkin, she left the room without a word.

Iris continued to eat as though nothing were amiss. After a few minutes, Jeremy excused himself and also left the room.

"She certainly knows how to clear a table," David said under his breath. "I'll give her that."

Bradlee picked up her glass and sipped her wine. When she realized Iris was now addressing her, she nearly choked. "I beg your pardon?"

Iris smiled. "I said I wonder if your mother would want to fly in for the party. I haven't seen her in ages."

Bradlee's mother and father under the same roof again? If Iris was looking for another disaster, she was headed in the right direction.

"I wouldn't count on that," Bradlee said. "Mother hates to fly, you know."

"It was just a thought." Iris turned to David. "Is there anyone you'd like to invite? Any close friends or business associates?"

His gaze lifted briefly to meet Bradlee's. "As a matter of fact, there are a number of people I'd like to be here when the announcement is made."

"Then you must put together a list for me." Iris dabbed her lips delicately with her napkin.

"Actually, I may need your help with the list," David said. "I'd like to invite everyone who was here the night I was kidnapped."

Iris froze with the napkin to her lips. Edward, who appeared to have drifted off, raised his head with a jerk, his expression one of horror. "That's impossible."

David stared back at him. "Why?"

"Because…" He looked to his mother for help.

"Because that was thirty-two years ago, my dear. Many of those people are dead."

"Well, that would narrow the guest list somewhat," David agreed. "But I would still like to have as many here as possible. Maybe we could go over the list together. If you can't find your copy, I'm sure I'll be able to come up with one from somewhere."

Iris's mouth thinned. Her blue eyes glinted dangerously. She was not used to being bested at her own game, and she didn't like it. "I'll see what I can do," she said coolly.

"Thank you." David stood. "Now, if you'll excuse us, Bradlee and I are going to take a walk in the gardens."

Bradlee looked up at him in surprise, then nodded, playing along. "It's a beautiful night and the gardens are lovely this time of year.…"

THE GARDENS *WERE* LOVELY. A full moon rose majestically over the treetops, lighting the deepest corners of the grounds with a soft, milky glow. The roses were still in bloom, and the sweet, heady scent drifted on the night wind. A moth fluttered past Bradlee's cheek, and she watched it for a moment, arrowing toward the brightly-lit terrace.

But where she and David stood, the light was filtered. Shadows slanted across his face, making him seem mysterious and exciting and more than a little dangerous.

"If you were aiming for shock value, I think you got your money's worth back there," she said. Although she had on a pale yellow sweater set with her soft, flowing skirt, she shivered in the cool evening air. Her hair tangled in the breeze, and she absently swept it behind her ears.

David shrugged. "I guess I just wanted to shake things up a little. See how they'd react."

"Did you really mean what you said? About having the same people who were here that night come to your party?"

"Can you think of a better way to draw out Colter's accomplice?"

"You're setting yourself up as bait," Bradlee said accusingly. "I don't think it's such a good idea."

"Why not?"

"You said yourself, the person we're looking for could be dangerous."

She saw him smile in the darkness. "So can I, if it comes to that."

Her chill deepened, but it wasn't just from the breeze. Bradlee realized again how very little she knew about David. He was a stranger and yet she'd been waiting all her life for him to come home.

They fell silent for a few minutes, then David nodded toward the mansion. "Are they always like that?"

"Like what?"

His tone was grim. "At each other's throats."

Bradlee grimaced. Dinner had been extremely uncomfortable for her, too. "It was better when Andrew was alive. Iris adored him. He could always make her laugh."

"Somehow I can't imagine ever doing that," David murmured.

"And Andrew's wife was a doll," Bradlee said. "Iris was devoted to her."

David turned to her. "What was she like?"

"Hope? Very sweet, very quiet, very elegant." Bradlee paused. "Actually, you've met her husband. Her *new* husband."

"She's married again?" He gave a short laugh, one without humor. "That didn't take long."

"Long enough. She and Andrew's marriage was rocky for a long time, and she and Jake go back a long way."

"Jake?"

"Jake McClain. The private detective who found you."

Bradlee sensed rather than saw his surprise. "Jake McClain is married to my brother's widow?"

"They were high-school sweethearts. When they broke up, Hope married Andrew. She stayed here for a while after he died, to be with Iris, and then later, she hired Jake to investigate the man claiming to be you." Bradlee paused. "During the course of the investigation, I guess they found their way back to each other."

"How romantic."

"Don't be cynical," she scolded. "I think it would

be wonderful to have a love like that. A love that never dies, no matter what.''

''I don't think there is such a thing.''

Bradlee stared up at him in reproach. ''You don't think there's one special person out there for each of us? You don't think it takes fate and maybe a little luck for us to find that person?'' She drew a long breath. ''Oh, but when we do...''

''When we do, what?'' She couldn't see his expression, but she could imagine one dark brow rising in skepticism. ''Fireworks? Explosions? The earth moves?''

''Yes,'' Bradlee agreed. ''All of that.''

''So what happens if we *don't* find that person?'' he asked. ''What if the fates are against us or our luck runs out?''

She thought about that for a second. ''Then I think we can love someone else. Maybe we can even be happy with someone else. But there's only one person out there who can be the love of our life.''

He was still staring down at her in the darkness. Bradlee sensed that something was different about him. Something had changed for him—an awareness that had caught him by surprise.

There was a touch of regret in his voice when he spoke. ''Love rarely works out the way we want it to, Bradlee. Real life is not a storybook fantasy.''

''But why can't it be?'' she asked. ''Why can't we have the fairy tale?''

''I think you're asking the wrong person that question.''

"I don't think so," she said softly. "If anyone deserves a happy ending, it's you."

There was suddenly an electric pause. Bradlee shivered as she stared up at him. He reached out and touched her hair. "I don't think I've ever known anyone like you."

She tilted her head to gaze up at him, and for a moment, they remained that way, no more than a heartbeat apart. And then slowly, David's head lowered and he touched his lips to hers.

It was hardly a kiss at all. No more than a feathery caress, but Bradlee felt it all the way to her soul. When he lifted his head, she murmured, "Don't stop." When he would have pulled away, she wrapped her arms around his neck and drew him back to her. Rising on tiptoe, she pressed her mouth to his, letting her tongue slip inside, grazing the edges of his teeth and beyond.

His reaction was immediate. He groaned against her lips, and his arms came around her, lifting her, holding her so close their bodies were almost one. In another minute, Bradlee hoped they would be.

She'd never experienced anything like this. His arms around her. His mouth on hers. His body against hers. It was almost a spiritual awareness of each other—a rightness that spiraled through every nerve-ending inside Bradlee. She wanted him and he wanted her. After all these years, after all they'd been through, what could be more perfect? What could be more destined?

Abruptly he broke the kiss, and Bradlee felt herself

sliding back down to earth. He forced their bodies apart, holding her at arm's length as he stared down at her, his expression serious.

"There's something I have to tell you."

Bradlee tried to calm her racing heart, tried to appear as though she experienced mind-blowing kisses every day. "What is it?"

He hesitated, then his hands dropped from her arms. Bradlee felt as if they were suddenly a million miles apart. "I don't have a right to kiss you like that."

"You do if I give you that right."

"You don't understand." He ran a hand through his dark hair, glanced away from her. "There's someone else."

Bradlee couldn't have heard him right. She thought he'd said there was someone else, but he couldn't have, because...

"Someone else?" she murmured.

"I'm engaged."

The bottom dropped out of Bradlee's world. She struggled for breath. "Engaged?"

"Her name is Rachel. She's an attorney. We met at a charity function a few months ago. We started seeing each other and...got engaged."

"Engaged."

He rubbed the back of his neck, looking distinctly uncomfortable. "Look, I'm sorry. I didn't mean to give you the wrong impression. I shouldn't have kissed you like that."

"Oh, well..." was about all Bradlee could muster. She shrugged.

He glanced down at her. "From now on, maybe it would be best if we...you know, keep our distance."

Bradlee's gaze flew to his. Keep their distance? That was the last thing she wanted. Didn't he know that? Couldn't he see that?

I'm thirty-five years old. I can't wait for you forever! she wanted to scream.

But instead she said calmly, "If we're going to find out who was in the nursery that night, we'll have to see each other occasionally. We'll have to talk."

"Not if you leave all this to me." He turned back to her in the darkness. For a moment, Bradlee thought he was going to take her in his arms again, but he didn't touch her, and she suddenly felt bereft. "I never wanted you involved in this in the first place. It's too dangerous."

"It's more dangerous for you than for me," she reminded him. "No one except you and Dr. Scott know I've been having the nightmares again. There's no reason for anyone to suspect I know anything."

His tone hardened. "And I'd like to keep it that way. From now on, let me handle this in my own way."

"But I have an appointment with Dr. Scott on Monday," Bradlee said. "You don't want to go with me?"

"I don't want *you* to go. Whatever secrets you

have locked inside your head are probably best left there.''

She gazed up at him accusingly. "You don't believe that.''

He shrugged. "I don't know what I believe anymore. All I know is that my life has changed so much in the last six weeks, I hardly recognize myself. Sometimes I wonder if David Powers even exists anymore.''

"Would it be so terrible to become Adam Kingsley?''

He turned to stare at the mansion, a looming shadow in the nightscape. "I think it might be.''

"You wouldn't have to be like them,'' she said softly.

"But what if I am?'' His gaze met hers, and in the moonlight, Bradlee saw something in his eyes that made her shiver.

SHE STOOD ON THE BALCONY off her room in the mansion and gazed down at the garden. Was he still down there somewhere? Was he thinking about *her,* the woman he was engaged to?

He'd called her Rachel, and the name summoned up an image of a beautiful seductress. She was an attorney, he'd said, so she was also smart and sophisticated. Bradlee could understand why he would be attracted to a woman like that—a woman his equal in every way—but...was he in love with her?

There had been nothing in his voice to indicate that he was. No softness when he spoke of her. No huskiness when he said her name. He might have been telling Bradlee about a business associate. But Rachel was his fiancée. They were engaged to be married.

Engaged.

The word had never sounded so final.

You're being ridiculous, she told herself, closing her eyes as the night wind drifted across her face. *You don't even know him.*

She was thirty-five years old. It was high time she stopped believing in fairy tales.

Maybe it was as her father had said at lunch. She'd always had some sort of fixation on Adam Kingsley. The kidnapping and her subsequent nightmares had made it impossible for her to forget him. That was all this was. Some sort of regression because he'd finally come home.

Keep telling yourself that, a little voice taunted her. *You might actually start to believe it.*

Chapter Eight

In spite of everything David had told her, Bradlee
was determined to keep her appointment with Dr.
Scott three days later.

This wasn't just about him, she reasoned. The kidnapping had affected her life in ways she was only
now beginning to understand. The nightmares, her
parents' divorce, and the underlying fear of being
kidnapped herself had left her deeply traumatized.
She'd put her life on hold for years because she'd
been terrified of trusting the wrong person.

But it was David who had been taken from his
home, David who had been raised by a stranger, David who had been manipulated and lied to. It was
David who had the most at stake here.

As much as Bradlee wanted to understand what he
was going through, she knew she would never be
able to. How could anyone? The only thing she could
do for him was to help him learn the truth. In some
ways, she needed that truth as much as he did. Perhaps that would be the one thing to give her the
closure she'd never been able to attain.

Dr. Scott greeted her at the door, ushered her into the office, and they got started right away. This time the hypnosis went even more smoothly because Bradlee knew what to expect. The moment Dr. Scott began to speak, Bradlee felt herself relax. The next thing she knew, she was sitting up on the couch, trying to smother a yawn.

"What happened?"

"You still couldn't identify the shadow, I'm afraid."

Bradlee frowned. She felt a little disoriented, not at all like she had the last time. "What do you think that means, Dr. Scott? Will I ever be able to remember?"

Dr. Scott stood and moved back to her desk. "Perhaps. But you have to face the very real possibility that you won't remember. That you'll never be able to put a face on that shadow."

That wasn't exactly what Bradlee wanted to hear. She licked her lips nervously. "Why?"

Dr. Scott sat down behind her desk, as if putting a barrier between them. "Because the shadow may not be a real person. It may simply be—as I've always thought—a manifestation of your terror."

"But why have the nightmares come back now?" Bradlee asked. Rather than feeling relaxed, the session had drained her this time. She pushed herself up off the couch. "Why am I seeing that shadow now, after all these years?"

"Because Adam Kingsley has been found." Dr. Scott studied Bradlee intently. "And because you still have emotions and fears you've never dealt with.''

"You don't know how much I wish that were true." Bradlee massaged her temples with her fingertips. "But I don't think it is. I think that shadow is very real, and unless I can remember who it represents, unless I can remember who was in the nursery that night, I'm very much afraid Adam Kingsley's life will be in danger.''

She started to leave, but when she got to the door, Dr. Scott called her name. Bradlee glanced back.

The psychiatrist was staring at her worriedly. "Are you all right?''

"I'm fine. Why?''

"You seem a bit...dazed.''

"I'm just disappointed," Bradlee said. "I really wanted to remember.''

"Try not to be so hard on yourself," Dr. Scott advised. "There may not be anything *to* remember.''

BRADLEE LEFT DR. SCOTT'S office and was almost to the elevators when she realized she'd forgotten to make another appointment. She hesitated. She really wasn't feeling very well, and the thought of getting out of the building into fresh air and sunshine was suddenly very appealing. But she knew if she left now she would just have to call later for the appointment, so she turned and retraced her steps down the corridor.

The receptionist had stepped away from her desk when Bradlee returned, and there were no other patients in the outer office. Dr. Scott's door was slightly ajar, and Bradlee crossed the carpeted floor to knock. As she lifted her hand, she heard voices coming from the inner office. She thought at first the psychiatrist was with a patient and she started to turn away. But then Dr. Scott's voice rose in anger, and Bradlee paused in spite of herself.

"Look, I'm telling you the truth. She hasn't remembered anything. You have nothing to worry about."

There was a pause, then, "I did what you told me, but I don't like it. I'm a doctor, for God's sake."

Bradlee's heart pounded as she stood outside the door listening. Was Dr. Scott talking about *her?*

"Convincing Mary to move away with her back then was one thing, but this—"

A noise in the hallway alerted Bradlee that the receptionist was on her way back. As quietly as possible, Bradlee crossed the room and stepped out into the hallway. The receptionist was returning from the copy room and nodded as they passed in the corridor. Bradlee smiled and then hurried toward the elevators. When the doors slid open, she rushed inside, then leaned against the wall, eyes closed, head reeling as the car descended to the lobby.

"Convincing Mary to move away with her back then was one thing, but this—"

She had to have been talking about Bradlee's mother, Mary Fitzgerald. It would be too much of a coincidence to think otherwise, especially considering the other part of the conversation Bradlee had overheard. *"Look, I'm telling you she hasn't remembered anything. You have nothing to worry about."*

Who had Dr. Scott been talking to?

Bradlee put a hand to her mouth. The implication of that conversation was terrifying. Dr. Scott had convinced Bradlee's mother to move away with her—not for Bradlee's well-being, but because someone had somehow coerced her into doing so. Just as someone was pressuring her now to make sure Bradlee didn't remember. *"I did what you told me, but I don't like it. I'm a doctor, for God's sake."*

What did you do? Bradlee's mind screamed.

This time when she'd come out of the hypnotic trance, she hadn't remembered anything about the session. She hadn't felt relaxed and refreshed, but disoriented and confused. What had Dr. Scott done to her while she'd been under?

Bradlee trembled all over. She didn't think she'd ever felt so vulnerable. So betrayed. So manipulated.

Her life had been torn apart back then. She'd been uprooted from her home, separated from her father, and why? Because someone had wanted her gone. Someone had wanted her out of the way because of what she might have seen the night of the kidnapping. She'd always thought her parents' divorce was all her fault, but now it seemed to have been part of a deadly scheme.

For the first time, Bradlee had an inkling of what David must have felt when he'd learned the truth of his identity. The two of them had been nothing more than pawns in someone's sick game back then. But who? Who was behind the manipulations? Who was the shadow in Bradlee's nightmares?

Out on the street, she paused, gulping in the fresh air, hoping it would clear her head, but her thoughts whirled chaotically. She wondered again what Dr. Scott might have done to her while she'd been under, and suddenly Bradlee couldn't wait to get miles away, put as much distance as she could between herself and the psychiatrist.

Her car was parked a few blocks away, and by the time Bradlee got there, she was breathing heavily. Her hands were clammy as she opened the door and slid behind the wheel. Starting the powerful engine of the Porsche, she merged into traffic. A horn sounded behind her and Bradlee glanced in the mirror, realizing she'd pulled out in front of someone.

Her hands gripped the wheel. *Concentrate*, she told herself. *Don't think about what happened. About what you heard.*

For a while it worked. She concentrated on her driving, but then the queasiness she'd been experiencing since she'd come out of the trance deepened. Her head spun dizzily, and Bradlee started to panic. She had no business being behind the wheel of a car. The last thing she wanted to do was hurt someone, but the thought of maneuvering the Porsche through lanes of traffic in order to pull over was terrifying.

Horns blared all around her. Cars passed in colorful blurs of confusion. Bradlee had no idea where she was going, only that she had to get off the road.

She veered across the center line, and tires

screamed behind her. Whipping the car back into her own lane, she somehow managed to merge right and ease the car to the curb. She killed the engine and sat with her stomach churning and her head spinning wildly out of control. She'd never felt so sick. Or so frightened.

She didn't know how long she'd remained like that, eyes closed, head against the steering wheel, when she became conscious of someone knocking on her window. With an effort, she lifted her head to gaze at the policeman peering down at her.

Bradlee rolled down her window and he bent to gaze inside the car. "What seems to be the problem, miss?"

"I'm sick," Bradlee told him. "It hit me all of a sudden. I had to pull over."

He glanced at her sternly. "You haven't been drinking, have you?"

"No, I'm just sick...." Her words trailed off, but something in her face must have convinced him.

He gave her a sympathetic nod. "You need to go to the hospital?"

"No, I'll be fine. I just need a minute."

"I don't want to leave you here like this, and you shouldn't be driving in your condition. Is there someone I can call?"

Bradlee thought for a moment. "You can call a friend of mine. He'll come get me." She gave him David's cell-phone number, praying he had his phone with him wherever he was.

The policeman went back to his car and placed the

call. After a few moments, he came back to Bradlee's window. "He's on his way. I suggested he take a cab so he can drive your car home. It wouldn't be a good idea to leave a vehicle like this parked out here," he said, admiring the Porsche. "You going to be okay now?"

Bradlee nodded weakly. "I'm feeling much better. Thanks for all your help."

The officer smiled. "Your friend sounded pretty worried about you. I think he'll take good care of you when he gets here."

"Thanks again," she murmured.

In her mirror, she watched him walk back to his car, get in, and pull out onto the street. Bradlee suddenly felt very alone and very vulnerable.

She glanced around. She was in a run-down area of town she didn't recognize, and she had no recollection of having driven there. The houses were small and dilapidated, the yards overgrown and crowded with rusty car parts and toys. Two young men wearing baggy jeans and tattered T-shirts stood on the sidewalk staring at her car and talking in low tones. Bradlee hurriedly rolled up her window and locked the doors.

It was hot inside the car, but she was shivering. She was alone and afraid and the sick spell had left her weak. What had happened to her? What had Dr. Scott done to her while she'd been under hypnosis? Drugged her?

A shudder ripped through her. The idea that Dr. Scott, a woman she'd trusted with her innermost thoughts and fears, had given her something to make her sick and disoriented, knowing she would be getting behind the wheel of a car—

Bradlee put her shaking hands to her face. Was it possible? Had Dr. Scott tried to *kill* her? And if so, why? Whom was she working for? Who wanted Bradlee dead?

She glanced at the two men on the sidewalk. Was it her imagination or were they edging closer? Did they want to hurt her, too?

You're being paranoid, Bradlee scolded herself, and tried to calm her racing heart. But when she saw a yellow cab turn onto the street just ahead of her, she'd never felt so relieved.

David got out of the taxi and strode toward her. He tried to open her door, but it was still locked and Bradlee struggled for a moment to release it.

When the lock clicked open, David drew back the door and knelt beside Bradlee. "Hey, you okay?"

She wanted nothing more than to tumble from the car into his arms. Instead she nodded. "I'm sorry to bother you. The policeman wouldn't let me drive, and I couldn't think of anyone else to call."

"It's okay. I'm glad he called me." He gazed at her with open concern, and Bradlee suddenly wanted to weep. He cared about her. He couldn't deny that. She could see it in his face.

"What happened?" he asked softly. When she didn't respond right away, she felt his hand against her hair, wiping it gently back from her damp forehead. "Bradlee?"

"I just felt sick. Dizzy. I had to pull over."

His hand was still in her hair, soothing her. "Do you need to see a doctor?"

"No. I don't want to see a doctor."

He paused. "All right. Why don't I take you back to the house, then?"

"I don't want to go there, either," she said. "At least, not right now."

"Look, I think you'd better tell me what happened." His tone brooked no argument. Bradlee glanced at him. His expression had deepened, hardened. His hand dropped from her hair.

She shivered. "I think Dr. Scott drugged me," she said. "David—" Her breath caught in her throat as fear swept over her again. "I think she tried to kill me."

"WHAT? WHAT THE HELL are you talking about?"

Bradlee drew a ragged breath. "I think she drugged me while I was under. She must have known I'd be driving—"

"Damn it!" he exploded. "You shouldn't have gone to see her alone."

"But you said we should keep our distance—"

He swore under his breath. "I know what I said. I also told you I didn't want you going to see Dr. Scott at all. I was afraid something like this might happen."

"But I'm all right," Bradlee protested. "And maybe nothing did happen. Maybe I just got sick."

"You said she tried to kill you," David reminded her.

"I know."

"What happened, Bradlee?"

She put her hands to her pale cheeks and closed her eyes. "When I came out of the trance, I couldn't remember anything. And I felt sort of...disoriented. Not rested like I did the last time. Dr. Scott said I didn't remember anything. She implied she didn't think there was anything for me *to* remember."

"Go on."

"When I got out into the hallway, I realized I hadn't made another appointment. So I went back." She paused. "I overheard her on the telephone in her office. She said she'd done what she'd been told, but she didn't like it. And then she said something like, 'Convincing Mary to take her away back then was one thing, but this...'"

She trailed off, shivering, and as David stared at her pale, frightened face, he didn't think he'd ever felt so helpless as he did at that moment. Or so enraged. He wanted nothing more than to drive back to Dr. Scott's office and confront the woman, make her tell them the truth.

Who paid you to betray a patient? Who paid you to screw up a three-year-old child's life?

Damn her, he thought. *Damn her to hell.*

Right now, however, his main concern was for Bradlee. Her color was coming back and she appeared to be feeling better. But there was still something in her eyes—a kind of dazed fear—that made

David want to pull her into his arms and hold her there forever. The thought that her life had been threatened because of him...because she wanted to help him...

My little guardian angel, he thought with an unexpected tenderness. Only she wasn't so little anymore. She was a grown woman and he was a man, and he was the one who wanted to do the protecting now.

The attraction he'd felt for Bradlee from the start had never been stronger than at this moment. She lifted her gaze to his, and slowly the fear in her eyes turned to something else. Before he could stop himself, before he could listen to the warning inside his head, David reached out and took her hand, drawing her fingers to his lips.

She sighed deeply, the sound going straight to his soul.

"You don't know how glad I am to see you," she whispered.

"Why did you come here?" he asked, glancing around at the shabby neighborhood. The two men who'd been eyeing her car had long since vanished.

Bradlee shrugged. "I don't know. All I remember is being sick and dizzy and knowing I had to get off the road before I hurt someone. Thank God, I didn't."

"Thank God *you* didn't get hurt," he murmured. He released her hand and stood. "What do you say we get out of here?"

"As long as you're driving."

He raised a dark brow. "Are you kidding? I've been wanting to see what this baby could do ever since I first saw her."

"No fancy stuff," Bradlee warned. "I've had enough stunt driving for one day." When she tried to stand, her legs were still shaky. David took her arm and helped her around to the passenger side of the car. Then he climbed in and started the engine.

He glanced over and found her staring at him. "What's the matter?"

"I don't know. You."

He cocked his head slightly. "What about me?"

"You look right at home behind that wheel."

He grinned. "I've handled a Porsche or two in my day."

"I can tell." She was still staring at him, her eyes glinting with something he couldn't quite define.

"What?"

She shook her head. "It's just that... I don't know. You look very Kingsley-like, all of a sudden."

BRADLEE THOUGHT FOR A while they were driving around aimlessly, but then she realized they were in east Memphis, near the airport. "Where are we going?"

David glanced at her. "I'm debating whether or not to take you to a hospital."

Bradlee sat up in alarm. "I'm feeling better, almost back to normal. What good would it do to go to the hospital now?"

"If Dr. Scott gave you a drug, don't you think we

need to know what it is? And how she administered it?"

"It was probably some sort of sedative. I don't think the drug itself was meant to hurt me. Besides, we can't prove she gave me anything. If we go to the hospital or to the police, she might find out about it, and I'd rather she not know we're on to her."

"We can't let her get away with this."

The darkness in his voice made Bradlee shiver. "I know. But...I don't want to go back there. I don't want to have to deal with any of this right now."

David dragged a hand through his hair. "This should never have happened to you. You should have stayed out of it."

"But I couldn't," Bradlee said. "Don't you see? I was lied to, too. I was used and manipulated, just like you were. What they did back then affected my life in ways I'm just now beginning to understand. That's why I've never been able to trust anyone. Why I've never been able to commit to anyone. Unlike you," she added, almost under her breath.

"Bradlee—"

"Look, don't tell me not to get involved. I am involved, okay? And I can take care of myself, so don't worry about me."

He spared her a glance at that. "Like you took care of yourself earlier?"

"I'm still here, aren't I?"

He shook his head helplessly. "You are without a doubt the most stubborn woman I've ever known."

More stubborn than Rachel? she wanted to ask.

But she didn't want to think about Rachel at all. Didn't want to know about the woman who would soon be David's wife.

He pulled into a slot in the short-term parking lot at the airport and shut off the engine.

"Why are we at the airport?" Bradlee asked.

He hesitated, then said, "It's like this. There's a flight leaving for St. Louis at one o'clock. I plan to be on it."

"Who's in St. Louis?" she asked in alarm. Rachel?

"Jenny Arpello. Do you remember her?"

Bradlee stared at him for a long moment. "The nanny?"

"She's agreed to see me—*us*—this afternoon."

"Us?"

David nodded but he still looked doubtful. "If you're up to it."

"How on earth did you find her?" Bradlee asked in amazement. "She left Memphis over thirty years ago."

He shrugged. "I have my ways. So are you coming with me or not?"

"Just try to keep me away," Bradlee told him.

"I've already tried that," he said dryly. "It didn't work."

Chapter Nine

Jenny Arpello lived on the outskirts of St. Louis, in a white frame house in serious need of a paint job. She was sitting on the front porch when they arrived and rose to greet them as they got out of the cab and walked up the cracked sidewalk to her house.

She had been a young woman thirty-two years ago, and lovely from the pictures Bradlee had seen of her. But she hadn't aged gracefully. She looked thin and haggard, the signs of an unkind life deeply etched into her face. But her blue eyes sparkled with excitement when she saw them.

She embraced them both, first David and then Bradlee. "I can't believe it," she said, wiping her eyes with the hem of her cotton apron. "Look at the two of you, together again after all this time. You always were inseparable."

With an arm around each of them, she ushered them into a living room that was neat but sparse. There were no pictures of children or grandchildren gracing walls and tabletops. No personal mementos to reveal the life Jenny Arpello might have led.

The barren house made Bradlee sad.

Jenny seated them on the sofa next to each other, then bustled off to the kitchen to bring back freshly squeezed lemonade and peanut-butter cookies still warm from the oven. "Your favorites," she said, beaming down at them. "I remembered."

When she'd seated herself across from them, she couldn't stop looking at David. Her eyes grew moist again. "I thought you were dead," she said. "To see you here like this…" Overcome with emotion, she dabbed at her eyes again.

David cleared his throat, as if unsure how to proceed. Finally he said, "We'd like to ask you some questions about that night."

"Of course. I'll tell you anything I can. I've relived it in my mind so many times it still seems like yesterday."

To get her started, David asked a few specific questions, but then, after a while, she needed no prompting. Stopping to wipe the moisture from her eyes every so often, she told them all she could remember about that night, about Edward and Pamela and Iris coming into the nursery to say good-night. About finding the hallway door open and assuming Bradlee's mother had been in to see Bradlee. About remembering to check the balcony doors before she went to bed.

"Are you absolutely certain the doors were locked before you went to bed?" David asked her.

"Absolutely. I remember checking to make sure because I'd had this premonition all day."

"Premonition?" Bradlee asked.

She nodded hesitantly. "It runs in my family. Sometimes I can sense when something bad is about to happen. I had the strongest feeling all day long that day."

"Did you tell anyone about it?" David asked.

Jenny's eyes teared again. "You don't know how many times I've wished I had. Maybe something could have been done to stop that monster, but as it was, I didn't think anyone would believe me. And I was so very afraid of Iris back then."

"Why?" David's voice sharpened.

"Your grandmother was a very powerful woman. The most formidable person I'd ever known. The staff were all terrified of her."

"What about my father?" David asked. "What do you remember about him?"

Jenny shifted uncomfortably, not able to meet his eyes. "He was very handsome and charming. Very ambitious."

It was hard to imagine those words describing the Edward Kingsley Bradlee knew now.

"He was also a bit impulsive," Jenny added. "Not one to think things through too well before he acted."

"You mean his marriage to Pamela?" David asked.

Jenny's lips thinned. "That woman should never have been brought into the house. She should never have been allowed around you boys."

"Why?"

Jenny glanced at David. "She had a cruel streak, that's why. I always had the feeling she could be abusive if she got half a chance."

David exchanged a look with Bradlee. "Did she ever hit Andrew or me?"

Jenny's eyes hardened. "I never actually saw her, but I suspected she'd done something to you the day of the kidnapping. She'd been into the playroom to see Jeremy, and when I came in, you were very upset. Andrew said she'd hit you."

"Did you confront her?" Bradlee asked, her tone a little more accusatory than she intended.

Jenny didn't seem to take offense. "I would have," she said. "I was all set to have it out with her the day after the fund-raiser, regardless of whether or not I lost my job. But then, Adam was taken and everything became a nightmare after that. I was questioned by the police, and I know for a while, the Kingsleys suspected I had something to do with the kidnapping. Why else did I not hear the intruder that night? I've asked myself that same question a thousand times. I knew something was wrong. I *knew* it. Why didn't I stay up? I only meant to lie down for a little while to rest. I was so keyed up, I didn't think I'd be able to sleep, but after I drank my warm milk, I must have dozed off. I didn't hear anything. It was as if I slept the sleep of the dead."

Bradlee glanced at David. His expression looked grim and forbidding. "Did you always drink warm milk before you went to bed?"

Jenny nodded. "Almost always. I had a hard time

sleeping back then. Still do. There was a little kitchenette off the nursery where I used to heat it up."

"Did anyone know about this particular habit of yours?"

Jenny shrugged. "I never made a secret of it. One of the maids remarked to me once that I should borrow some of Pamela's sleeping pills. But I would never take any kind of drugs while children were under my care."

Maybe it was because her own recent experience was still so fresh in her mind, but the talk of drugs made Bradlee uneasy. "Is it possible someone in the house that night put something in your milk?" she asked.

Jenny looked shocked. Her gaze met first Bradlee's, then David's before she slowly asked, "Why are you two really here? What's going on?"

If possible, David's expression grew even more grim. "We have reason to believe someone in the house that night may have helped Raymond Colter kidnap me."

Jenny's eyes rounded with shock. Her right hand went to her heart. "Oh, dear God, are you saying one of the Kingsleys had you kidnapped? Their own flesh and blood?"

"Not necessarily. There were a lot of people at the fund-raiser that night. Any one of them could have come upstairs, unlocked the balcony doors, and then signaled to Colter in the gardens. They may even have drugged your milk, as Bradlee suggested, to make sure you wouldn't hear anything."

Jenny closed her eyes. The hand at her heart shook badly. "All these years I've blamed myself. All these years I've regretted falling asleep that night more bitterly than you can imagine. I let a child in my care be taken by a stranger. I thought he'd killed you. Murdered you in cold blood. Do you know what it's been like, living with that guilt?"

"YOU'RE AWFULLY QUIET," David said on the flight back to Memphis. Bradlee hadn't spoken two words since they'd left Jenny's house. She was obviously upset and he thought he knew why.

She leaned her head against the seat back, as if overcome with exhaustion. "I feel so sorry for her. She's so alone."

"I know."

Bradlee turned to stare at him and her gaze hardened. "It's because of the kidnapping, you know. Because of what they did."

"Colter and his accomplice, you mean."

"How could anyone be that cold-blooded, David? How could anyone take a child from his home, his family, hold him for ransom, let everyone think he was dead? Raymond Colter was a monster, but at least he was a stranger. To think that someone we know may have been behind your kidnapping is almost more than I can comprehend. What happens when we find out who this person is?"

"What do you mean?" David didn't like the strange glint in her eyes. He should never have brought her with him to see Jenny. But after her session with Dr. Scott, after what she'd overheard, he wasn't about to leave her behind.

"I mean, how do we deal with a betrayal like that?"

David shrugged. "Look, my mother said someone connected to the Kingsley family paid Colter to kidnap me. That doesn't mean it was a member of my family, or even anyone closely related. There were a lot of people in the house that night, Bradlee."

"I know. And something my father told me the other day keeps bothering me. He said Edward was trailing badly in the polls because of his marriage to Pamela. He said Edward's political rival, a man named Cotton Weathers, admitted leaking the story about Edward's affair with Pamela while your mother was still alive to the press, hoping to ruin Edward's bid for governor. And it almost worked. Then you were kidnapped, and my uncle decided to use your abduction to their advantage. He played on voter sympathy and it worked. Edward was elected."

"Are you saying you think your uncle may have had something to do with it?"

She glanced at him sharply. "Actually, no. I was thinking about Cotton Weathers."

"But you just said my kidnapping helped get my father elected."

"Yes, but maybe Cotton's plan backfired. Maybe he thought kidnapping one of Edward's sons would cause him to pull out of the race."

"It's possible. But if my kidnapping was politically motivated, I'd be more inclined to believe that someone already knew, or at least had a pretty good idea, what the consequences would be. That my kidnapping would put voters' sympathy squarely in Edward's corner. And who would be in a better position to know that than Edward Kingsley himself?''

Bradlee gasped. ''You think your own father paid to have you kidnapped?''

David shrugged. ''I don't know anything about the man. But Jenny said he was ambitious back then, and from everything I've read about them, the Kingsleys don't like to lose.''

''But he only served two terms as governor and then retired from politics,'' Bradlee said. ''Why would he risk so much, only to give it all up a few years later?''

David turned in his seat to face her. ''I've thought about that. Maybe the guilt got to him. Think about it. Maybe I wasn't supposed to disappear like that. According to my mother, Colter said he had to return me to my family in a few days, but she took me away before he could. When everyone thought I was dead, imagine how that would have made my father—or whoever paid Colter to kidnap me—feel. And it certainly seems as though Edward has had something preying on his mind all these years. Look what he's done to himself.''

''I can't believe a father would do something like that to his own son,'' Bradlee said. She bit her lip, thinking. ''What about Pamela?''

''What about her?''

''Jenny said that Pamela had done something to

you the day of the kidnapping. Supposing she was worried what Edward would do when he found out.''

David frowned. ''So she paid Colter to kidnap me? She would have had to work awfully fast.''

''Not if she and Colter already knew each other.''

David remembered what Colter had told him, that he'd worked at the mansion as a security guard. Was it possible he and Pamela had had a relationship? Of all the people that David had met so far, it was easier to believe Pamela Kingsley had been behind his kidnapping than anyone else.

''Maybe she decided she could kill two birds with one stone,'' Bradlee said. ''She'd keep Edward from finding out that she'd been abusive to you, and she'd get rid of one of the Kingsley heirs standing in Jeremy's way.''

''Then why not get rid of both Andrew and me?'' David said, playing the devil's advocate.

Bradlee shrugged. ''Obviously, I don't have everything worked out.''

''There's still the possibility that whoever conspired with Raymond Colter did so out of nothing more than greed,'' David said. ''Maybe they split the ransom money. Don't forget, thirty years ago $250,000 was still a lot of money.''

''It wouldn't seem so for the high rollers who attended the fund-raiser that night,'' Bradlee said. ''Most of them were loaded. That's why they were invited.''

''Most of them may have appeared to be loaded,'' David said grimly. ''Any one of them, however, could have found himself—or herself—in just enough financial trouble that a quarter of a million dollars would have bailed him out.'' David, staring down at Bradlee, saw something flash in her eyes. Something that almost looked like fear. ''What's the matter?''

''Nothing,'' she said. ''Nothing.''

But David could tell that something he'd said had frightened her. Did she know more about that night than she was telling?

He didn't like to think so, but it came back to one thing: There wasn't a single person connected to the Kingsleys that he could truly trust.

Maybe not even his guardian angel.

UNABLE TO SLEEP THAT NIGHT, Bradlee took a midnight walk in the gardens. David had warned her about being alone, but she had to have fresh air. She had to try and clear her head because ever since they'd returned from St. Louis, a myriad of disturbing thoughts had been swirling around inside her.

''Most of them may have appeared to be loaded. Any one of them, however, could have found himself—or herself—in just enough financial trouble that a quarter of a million dollars would have bailed him out.''

''You were fighting about money the night Adam Kingsley was kidnapped.''

''Dammit, Mary, I told you I have everything under control.''

Bradlee closed her eyes. It wasn't possible, she

told herself. Her father had weaknesses, but he would never have been involved in Adam's kidnapping, no matter what kind of financial trouble he found himself in.

But what about her uncle? What about Harper Fitzgerald? Bradlee knew him to be brilliant, ambitious, and ruthless. He'd made millions as the man behind the scenes, pulling the strings offstage in order to get his candidate elected to public office. None of his clients had ever lost a single campaign. Bradlee was sure that was why the Kingsleys had hired him in the first place. They knew he would not let Edward lose.

"He called it the sympathy factor."

All this time Bradlee had been worried about what would happen if she and David found out someone in his own family had paid to have him kidnapped, but what if Raymond Colter's conspirator was someone in *her* family? What would David think of her then?

Would he wonder if she had been covering for them all these years? Would he believe her when she said she really couldn't remember who'd come into the nursery that night?

Bradlee turned to stare up at the mansion. In the moonlight, her gaze traveled over the imposing facade, pinpointing the balcony off the nursery. The windows beyond lay in darkness, but as Bradlee watched, she saw a beam of light through the French doors, as if someone were moving about in the nursery with a flashlight.

She took a step toward the house. Who could be up there? The nursery had been locked when she and David had tried to get in a few nights ago. If it was a member of the staff or the family, why not turn on the light? Why use a flashlight as if to avoid detection?

The flashlight went out suddenly, and Bradlee wondered if she had been spotted. She stared at the window for several more minutes, but the room remained dark, leaving her to think she might have imagined the whole thing.

Chapter Ten

The day after they returned from St. Louis, David told Bradlee he wanted to go see Dr. Scott, to try and persuade her to tell them who she had been working for back then, and who she was working for now. He used the word *persuade,* but Bradlee read *coerce* in his eyes. Maybe even *threaten.* She didn't want things to get out of hand, so she insisted on going with him, and David reluctantly agreed.

Knowing what she now knew, Bradlee dreaded the prospect of facing the psychiatrist again. The woman had been privy to her innermost thoughts and had betrayed her. Betrayed a three-year-old child who'd desperately needed her help.

What kind of woman—what kind of *doctor*—would do something like that?

Either a desperate one or a very frightened one, Bradlee thought with a shiver.

As if sensing her trepidation, David took her hand when they stepped out of the elevator. "I'm okay," she assured him. "I want to know who's behind this as much as you do."

"We're in this together now," he said, gazing down at her. "I didn't want you involved, but you were right. You already are involved, and the quicker we find out who's behind all this, the better I'll feel about your safety."

His concern touched Bradlee, but just as she was drawing to his warmth, he released her hand.

The receptionist was alone in the office, boxing up files. She appeared harried and somewhat distressed. She glanced up when they walked in and shoved a lock of hair from her forehead.

"Oh, Miss Fitzgerald. Did you have an appointment with Dr. Scott this morning? I thought I called all her patients—"

Bradlee shook her head, stopping the woman in mid-sentence. "I don't have an appointment. But I was hoping she'd have a minute to see me. It's important."

The receptionist returned to her job of sorting files. "I'm sorry, but Dr. Scott isn't in. She was called out of town on an emergency."

David said, "It looks as if you're cleaning out the office. Dr. Scott *is* coming back, isn't she?"

The receptionist glanced up with a frown. "I really can't say. All I know is that she called me at home last night to tell me she was leaving town. I was to come here and close up the office, box up all the files, and put them in storage. And then find myself another job," she added bitterly.

"Did she tell you where she was going?" Bradlee asked.

The receptionist cast a wary glance around the office. Then she lowered her voice. "That's the strange part. I don't even know where to send this stuff. She said she'd send me an address later."

Bradlee wished the woman luck on her job hunting, then she and David left the office. Out on the street, Bradlee asked, "What do you make of all that?"

David shrugged. "Evidently she panicked and decided to split before she got dragged into this thing any further. I would be surprised if she hasn't been planning for this little contingency for years."

"Meaning it's not going to be that easy to find her?"

"Exactly." His expression turned grim. "I'm not without resources, though. She can't have gotten too far. I'll see what I can do about getting the police to help us track her down."

"What if they find her, David? It'll be her word against mine that she drugged me. We can't prove anything. You were right. I should have gone to the hospital that day. At least we'd have that."

"We may not be able to prove anything, but if we scare her badly enough, she might be willing to talk."

"Raymond Colter wasn't. He swears to this day he didn't have a coconspirator."

Frowning, David stared at the flow of traffic on the street. "I know. But Dr. Scott has a lot more to lose than Colter. The threat of spending the rest of her life in prison might be enough to sway her."

But somehow Bradlee didn't think it would be. Whoever was behind the conspiracy wielded enough power that even the threat of prison wouldn't be enough to make Dr. Scott talk—if the woman was even still alive.

IRIS AND HER SECRETARY had been working on the invitations to David's "coming out" party for days. That afternoon, she summoned Bradlee to her sitting room, where she reclined on her green silk chaise, giving her secretary last-minute instructions for mailing. Since time was of the essence—the party was to be held at the end of the following week—most of the invitations would be hand-delivered by courier.

The secretary scurried out, instructions in hand, and closed the door behind her. Iris motioned Bradlee to a chair near her chaise.

"I've done as David asked," she said, once Bradlee was settled. Iris wore a blue satin bed jacket that deepened the color of her eyes. She handed Bradlee a sheet of paper with a typed list of names. "As long as you're here, I may as well give this to you. You can pass it on to him."

Bradlee glanced up. "What is this?"

"The guest list for the party. Although many of them are deceased and many others are scattered to the four corners of the earth, I've done my best to bring as many as I could back together."

"You've obviously gone to a great deal of trouble," Bradlee said. "Why don't you give this to David yourself?"

"You see more of him these days than I do," she said. "And I'd like for him to have it as soon as possible."

Bradlee shrugged, folding the list and slipping it into the pocket of her jeans. "I'll give it to him when I see him, then."

"Thank you." Iris adjusted the blanket spread over her legs. "You and he have become very close, haven't you? Almost like you've never been apart."

Bradlee couldn't tell if the old woman was pleased by this or not. With Iris, you could never be entirely sure—until the hammer fell. "I've tried to be his friend," Bradlee said. Her gaze was direct. "I think he needs one right now."

Iris nodded, a flicker of approval in her eyes. "You must wonder about our response to his arrival. It must seem as though we aren't overjoyed to have him home again."

When Bradlee said nothing, Iris continued. "But we are. Make no mistake about that. Having him here, safe and sound, is an answer to my prayers. For over thirty years, I mourned my grandson, and then to discover he was still alive, to have found him when all hope was lost..." She trailed off, her eyes shimmering with unexpected tears.

Bradlee leaned toward her. "Then why not tell him? Why not let him know what his being here means to you? It could make such a difference to him."

Iris's eyes closed briefly. "I want to. I want that more than anything. To take my grandson in my

arms, to hold him again as I did when he was little...'' Then her voice hardened, drawing shivers
down Bradlee's spine. ''You heard about the man
who came here a few months ago claiming to be
Adam, what he did to Andrew.''

Bradlee nodded.

''I opened my heart to Michael Eldridge. I thought
he was the answer to my prayers. I loved him the
moment I laid eyes on him. I brought him into my
home, gave him my devotion, and then to find out
he was an impostor, to discover he had helped murder my grandson...'' She lifted her chin, her eyes
glittering like sapphires. ''I cannot go through that
again.''

''But you *know* David is Adam. The DNA tests
proved that,'' Bradlee said.

''Michael Eldridge's DNA test proved *him* to be
Adam.''

''But it was faked. David's wasn't.''

''In my mind, I do know he is Adam,'' Iris replied
softly. ''But my heart is still very much afraid to
believe.''

Suddenly, the power and wealth and prestige
seemed to melt away from Iris Kingsley, leaving a
vulnerable old woman who was terribly afraid of being hurt again. For the first time in a long time, Bradlee felt her heart go out to her.

''You don't have to be afraid,'' she said. ''I know
he's Adam. I *know*.''

Iris's gaze lifted to meet Bradlee's. An understanding passed between them. "You've been waiting for him to come home, too, haven't you, my dear?"

"Since the night he disappeared," Bradlee said simply.

BACK IN HER OWN ROOM, Bradlee stared down at the list of names. She wanted to trust the pain and vulnerability she'd glimpsed in Iris's eyes earlier, wanted to believe the real reason no one in this house had welcomed David home was because they'd all been badly hurt.

But there had been something else in Iris's eyes, a slyness lurking behind the tears of sadness. Bradlee wanted to trust the old woman's sincerity, but Iris Kingsley was a woman of machinations. She never did anything without a reason.

Could they trust that the list contained the names of *all* those who had been present the night Adam was kidnapped? There was no reason Bradlee could think of for Iris and Edward not to have invited everyone, but she and David had only Iris's word for it.

What they needed, Bradlee decided, was another list, and she knew exactly where they could get one.

She'd worked in her Uncle Harper's office one summer after high school, and she remembered that he kept an extensive filing system, never threw any kind of paperwork away. He had a real thing about it.

The whole basement of his office building was used for file storage, and Bradlee would be willing to bet there would still be a copy of the guest list from Edward Kingsley's fund-raiser somewhere among the thousands and thousands of folders. The question was, would Harper willingly give her a copy?

Bradlee hadn't seen her uncle in years, but she remembered him as being secretive, almost paranoid at times. He'd always frightened her a little, and the prospect of seeing him again was daunting, even at her age. But she could think of no other way to get a copy of the guest list.

Opening the door of her bedroom, she stepped out into the hallway. Illiana was just coming out of David's room with a basket of cleaning supplies.

"Is he in?"

"No, Miss Fitzgerald. He left a little while ago."

"Did he say where he was going?"

The maid shook her head. "He said to tell you he'd see you later."

Bradlee thanked Illiana and then went back to her room. Where had he gone? And why hadn't he told her? He'd said they were in this together.

Since she didn't know where he'd gone, Bradlee had no idea what time he would be back. In the meantime, would it hurt to pay her uncle a little visit?

She thought about Harper on the way over to his office. In addition to being secretive and paranoid, she also remembered him as being cold and arrogant—not at all an easy man to talk to. The only reason he'd given her a job that summer was because her father had asked him to. Bradford had needed something to occupy his sulky teenage daughter while he made plans for his third—or had it been his fourth?—wedding.

As Bradlee pulled into the parking garage and parked, she tried to plan her course of action. Should she just come right out and ask her uncle for a copy of the guest list? He would probably deny such a list existed after thirty-two years, but Bradlee knew better. She remembered his secretary, a woman named Lucille Carver, grumbling more than once that summer that Bradlee's uncle never, ever threw out anything. And Bradlee had had the unenviable task of carting boxes of papers down to the basement and filing for hours at a time.

As she entered the building, she was astonished to see her uncle's secretary coming out. Lucille hadn't changed a bit, right down to the snug navy suit, low-heeled pumps, and tortoiseshell-frame glasses. Bradlee started to speak, but just then, Lucille saw someone on the street, waved, and hurried out.

Bradlee crossed the lobby to the receptionist's desk. "Hi," she said. "My name's Bradlee Fitzgerald. I'm here to see my uncle."

The receptionist glanced at her curiously. "He's not in, Miss Fitzgerald. He won't be back until two."

"That's okay," Bradlee improvised. "I just saw Lucille leaving. She doesn't mind if I wait in her office."

The receptionist shrugged. "Go on back, then."

Bradlee walked down a long corridor lined with offices, most of them closed and silent. Her uncle was obviously not involved in an active campaign at the moment, or all the offices in the building would be beehives of activity. As it was, the place appeared deserted and not a little forlorn.

Harper's office suite was located at the end of the hallway. Bradlee entered the outer office and stood gazing around. The door to the inner office was closed and more than likely locked. She remembered her uncle being a stickler for security. Lucille's desk was cleared away and the computer turned off. It looked as if she'd left for the day.

Bradlee casually wandered over to the desk. The summer she'd worked here she'd been assigned to help Lucille, primarily because Harper hadn't wanted to be bothered with Bradlee himself. Lucille had given her a number of duties to perform, but her primary job had been filing. For the first few weeks, Lucille had accompanied her to the basement, unlocked the door, then lumbered back upstairs to be at Harper's beck and call.

Even then, Lucille had not been a small woman and had soon tired of trooping up and down the stairs. She'd finally shown Bradlee where she kept the key to the file room, swearing her to secrecy. If Harper ever found out she'd entrusted that key to anyone—even his niece— Lucille warned, it could mean her job.

Sitting down at the secretary's desk, Bradlee ran her fingers along the ledge underneath. The key was still there, taped to the underside of the desk as if no one had ever thought of such a hiding place. Bradlee wondered what her uncle would say if he knew the key to his precious files had been hidden all these years in the place most commonly used by secretaries the world over.

Tearing away the tape, Bradlee withdrew the key and slipped it into her pocket. Then she crossed the room and hurried down the hall, quickly unlocking the door to the basement stairs. Slipping inside, she stood in pitch-darkness, sliding her hand along the wall until she found the light switch.

Even with the light on, the huge, cavernous room was creepy. Rows and rows of filing cabinets gave testament to her uncle's illustrious career managing successful political campaigns. It made Bradlee shudder to think of what secrets might be hidden in the depths of those files.

Five filing cabinets were devoted to the Kingsley campaign. Everything inside was color coded and meticulously cross-referenced by dates and subject matter. It only took her a few minutes to locate the folder dedicated to the fund-raiser.

Her fingers shaking, Bradlee withdrew the file and laid it on top of one of the cabinets. For a long moment, she simply stared at the folder, hesitating to open it. The label contained the date of June 24th, the night Adam had been kidnapped.

Taking a deep breath, she opened the folder and riffled through the contents. There was a copy of the invitation that had been sent out, along with press releases, a list of previous donors, including donation amounts—the more generous ones starred for future reference—and a myriad of other paperwork that had gone into the planning and preparation of the fund-raiser. Toward the back of the file, Bradlee found the list she'd been searching for.

There was a copy machine in the basement, and she hurried over, duplicating the list and then returning the original to the folder. She closed all the drawers and glanced around, making sure no one would know she'd been there.

Back in Lucille's office, she knelt to retape the key to the desk. Just as she was about to straighten, she heard voices out in the hallway coming toward Harper's office.

She recognized both voices instantly. Her uncle and her father were coming back from lunch, and by the sounds of it, they'd each had a few drinks.

Bradlee didn't have time to get up, so she slid under the desk and pulled the chair toward her.

Her father was speaking as they entered the office. "You know she's always had an obsession with that boy. Since he's come back, it's started up again. I don't think it's a good idea for the two of them to get so chummy. If she comes around asking you questions about the kidnapping, just don't say anything that'll encourage her."

She could hear Harper unlocking his office door. In a voice lower and colder than his brother's, he said, "Don't worry. I'll take care of it."

"It's for her own good," Bradlee's father said, almost defensively.

"You got that right."

She heard her uncle's office door close, then all was silent. After waiting a few seconds, Bradlee scurried out from under the desk and, as quietly as possible, slipped from the office.

COTTON WEATHERS WAS a bitter, cantankerous old man with dirty gray hair unbefitting his first name and faded, bloodshot eyes that seemed to stare right through David as the housekeeper ushered him into the study.

The desk the old man sat behind concealed his legs, but not the wheelchair. He dismissed the house-keeper with a crisp, backhanded wave.

"Who the hell did you say you are?" he thundered.

"My name is David Powers. I'm doing some research on the Kingsley kidnapping. I'd like to ask you a few questions."

The faded eyes narrowed, looking a lot more shrewd than David had originally thought. "What paper you with?"

David hadn't actually said he was a reporter, but he'd intentionally given the housekeeper that impression. "I'm from up north," he evaded.

"Don't have much use for Yankees," Cotton warned. "Never did. Ask your questions, then get the hell out."

"I'll make this as fast as I can," David said. "Mind if I sit?"

The old man grunted, which David took as permission. He sat down in a worn leather chair and faced Cotton Weathers. "You were Edward Kingsley's chief political foe back then, right?"

He grunted again, his expression one of disgust. "If it wasn't for his mother, that sumbitch couldn't have got himself elected dogcatcher."

"He was trailing in the polls until the kidnapping, wasn't he?" David prompted.

Cotton's eyes flared with a hatred unabated by thirty-two years. "Any decent man would have pulled out of the race, concentrated on finding his kid—but not Kingsley. Oh, no. He used his own son's murder as a ticket to the governor's mansion. I always did despise the man, but I couldn't stomach him after that."

"Why did you hate him so much?"

"His name was Kingsley, wasn't it?"

"What did you have against the Kingsleys back then?"

"That's my business," Cotton snapped. "My quarrel with them had no bearing on the kidnapping. That *is* what you came to talk about, isn't it? That's all anyone's been talking about since Raymond Colter confessed. Thank God the Kingsleys don't have someone running for office now. He'd be a shoo-in."

"I've been told you were the one who leaked the story of Edward's affair with Pamela Harrington to the press. You came to the fund-raiser that night to gloat. Any truth in that?"

Cotton shrugged. "There might be. The public had a right to know what kind of man he was. Unlike nowadays, character mattered back then. Least it did until his kid turned up missing."

"What did you think would happen when you heard about the kidnapping? Did you think Edward would pull out of the race?"

"Like I said, any decent man would have."

"Maybe you were counting on that." David watched Cotton's expression carefully, saw the darkening of his eyes and the hardening of his mouth. But to David's surprise, the old man laughed. It was an ugly sound, bearing little resemblance to humor.

"You're no more a reporter than I am. Who the hell are you?"

"You're right," David said. "I'm not a reporter, but I am investigating the kidnapping."

"You a cop?" His eyes flashed with something that might have been fear, but Cotton Weathers didn't appear to be a man easily frightened.

David shrugged without answering, letting the old man draw whatever conclusions he wanted. "In a few days, you'll be receiving an invitation to a party at the Kingsley estate in honor of her grandson, Adam Kingsley. I would highly recommend that you attend."

Cotton glared at him. "Why should I?"

"Everyone who was present at Edward Kingsley's fund-raiser than night is expected to attend—those who're still alive, that is. If you don't come, it might look as if you have something to hide."

David stood to leave, but before he got to the door, he heard a sound that made him whirl around. Cotton

Weathers had pushed the wheelchair back from his desk and was standing. He looked as steady as any twenty-year-old, and the gun aimed at David's heart didn't shake one bit.

"I don't know why you came here," he said, "but I do know this. Iris Kingsley is not the only one in this town with some clout. I could put a bullet in your heart right this minute and not spend a single night in jail. You believe that?"

"Obviously, you do," David said. "So I'm listening."

"You go back and tell Iris Kingsley I don't know what she's trying to pull, but I don't take orders from her. I never did and I never will. Unlike most everyone else in this town, I'm not afraid of that old battle-ax. And that royally pisses her off."

David, keeping an eye on the gun, said, "Anything else?"

Cotton Weathers stared at him for a long moment, relishing every second of his performance. Then slowly he lowered the weapon. "Yeah," he said. "There is one other thing. Welcome home…Adam."

Chapter Eleven

The night of David's party was mild and moonlit, but a front, still miles away, threatened rain for later that evening.

Dressed in a white Calvin Klein gown she'd bought especially for the occasion, Bradlee stepped onto the balcony off her room, lifting her face to the night sky. She tried to concentrate on the moonlight instead of the dark clouds gathering in the distance, but the coming storm seemed ominous to her. She thought about the premonition Jenny Arpello had experienced the day of the kidnapping, and a shiver of fear rippled through Bradlee.

Something bad was about to happen. She didn't know whether the feeling was a presage of things to come, or only her imagination, but suddenly Bradlee knew she and David would have to be on their guard. Tonight Raymond Colter's accomplice might very well return to the scene of the crime, and if they weren't careful, they could get caught in his trap once again.

DAVID, STRUGGLING WITH a cufflink, muttered an oath when someone knocked on his door. "Come in," he called, and Iris swept in, looking as regal as a queen on coronation day. She wore a midnight-blue gown with a satin train and a diamond-and-sapphire necklace that could easily have been a museum piece.

Her white hair gleamed in the light, and her blue eyes, almost the exact shade of her dress, gave him a careful scrutiny. She nodded briskly. "You look very handsome."

"Thank you." David managed the cufflink, then slipped on his tuxedo jacket.

"This will be quite a night," she said. Her voice was calm, but her eyes glittered with an emotion David couldn't define.

"Yes, I guess it will be," he said.

Iris hesitated. "I did what you asked. I contacted everyone who was here that night—everyone who is still alive, that is. Some of them don't have a clue as to why they've been invited."

"Everyone will know soon enough," David said.

"And what will you do when they know?" Iris said. "When all of this becomes public? Will you then feel as if you're Adam?"

David wasn't sure what he would feel. He hadn't thought beyond the announcement itself and observing the various reactions to it. Would he feel like Adam Kingsley when everyone knew about him? If so, what would happen to David Powers?

He glanced around the opulent room, far bigger

and more luxurious than his apartment in New York, and the woman who stood before him——his grandmother——wearing a gown and jewels the likes of which he hadn't seen even on Rachel, whose tastes had always seemed appallingly extravagant to him.

He didn't know how to be a Kingsley, and it suddenly seemed imperative to him that he not lose sight of who he was, of where he'd come from, of the way he'd been raised. A man's soul could easily get lost in their kind of wealth and power.

As if reading his mind, Iris said, "I have something for you."

David was immediately on his guard. "What is it?"

She pulled something from her beaded evening bag. "Hold out your hand."

He felt like a kid on Halloween, curious but more than a little wary. When his hand opened, Iris dropped a shiny gold medallion into his palm. David held it between his thumb and forefinger, lifting it to the light. One side bore an emblem stamped in the metal, but the other side was blank. A tiny hole had been punctured through the top to accommodate a chain.

"Do you know what that is?" Iris asked.

"It looks like some kind of coin but I don't recognize the stamp. I've never seen one like it."

"There's only one other like it in the world. They belonged to you and Andrew. Put together they make a whole. You were wearing yours the night you were kidnapped, and Andrew was wearing his the night he died.''

David caressed the smooth metal as a memory flashed in his mind: The chain had been ripped from his neck by his kidnapper. *"This is my proof, kid, in case they don't believe I have you."*

He glanced up at Iris. ''How did you get it back?''

''Raymond Colter had it in his possession all these years. When he confessed and was sent to prison, the coin was returned to me. And now I'm giving it back to you. I hope one day soon you'll want to wear it again.''

Gold chains weren't exactly his style, but there was something about the medallion—a connection to his past—that David had been looking for all his life. He closed his fingers around the cool metal. ''Thank you,'' he said.

Iris nodded, then turned and left the room.

THE BALLROOM LOOKED dazzling, with its glittering chandeliers, colossal arrangements of late-summer flowers, and ornate, gilded mirrors that reflected the stunning ball gowns worn by the female guests.

An orchestra had set up on the gallery overlooking the ballroom and was playing a melody hauntingly familiar to Bradlee. Nerves fluttered in her stomach as she stood just inside the doorway, gazing around.

The receiving line had already dispersed, and Iris had taken her position in a high-backed chair at the far end of the ballroom, away from the orchestra. She watched the proceedings with an expression Bradlee couldn't fathom. Was she wondering what effect her announcement later in the evening would have on the gathering?

Edward and Pamela were at Iris's side, but Pamela looked as if she would rather be almost anywhere else. She was dressed in a magnificent silver gown that, even though it had been designed for a much younger woman, still looked stunning on her.

But tonight her face gave away her age. Even the most skilled plastic surgeon would have a hard time erasing the deep worry lines etched across her brow, and Bradlee couldn't help wondering what secrets Pamela harbored concerning the night Adam was kidnapped.

As usual, Jeremy Willows stood apart from the family group, one hand nursing a drink while the other was shoved deep into the pocket of his tuxedo trousers. It was obvious to Bradlee that neither Jeremy nor his mother were enjoying the festivities, and her earlier feeling of dread came back to her. Not everyone present tonight would be happy that Adam Kingsley had returned. Now someone else stood between Jeremy and Iris's fortune.

The ballroom was warm, but Bradlee grew cold as her gaze swept the throng of guests. She spotted her father and Crystal among the dancers, and catching her glance, her father waved. But Bradlee thought he and Crystal didn't look particularly pleased to be here, either, and that was unusual for her father. This was his element. He loved working a crowd and adored showing off his new brides. Was there trouble in paradise already, or was something else—the evening itself, perhaps—causing her father's somber expression?

Bradlee remembered the conversation she'd overheard between him and her uncle. *"You know she's always had an obsession with that boy. Since he's come back, it's started up again. I don't think it's a good idea for the two of them to get so chummy. If she comes around asking you questions about the kidnapping, just don't say anything that'll encourage her."*

And her uncle's response had been, *"Don't worry. I'll take care of it."*

Take care of it how? Bradlee wondered. It was bad enough to think that someone in this room had hired Colter to kidnap David, worse still that it might have been someone in David's own family. But now to have doubts about *her* father and uncle…

Bradlee wanted to dispel those doubts, but the sight of her uncle heading across the ballroom toward her father only made them worse. Harper Fitzgerald had always been a man who dealt in secrets. He was nearing seventy now, with gray hair and leathered skin, but Bradlee didn't think that age had changed him much. He was still one of the most formidable-looking men she'd ever known, and she suspected he still didn't like to lose.

How far had he been willing to go thirty-two years ago to ensure Edward Kingsley's victory?

As Bradlee stood watching, she saw him approach her father who bent to say something to Crystal.

Then both men left the dance floor. Crystal was immediately surrounded by a swarm of men anxious to take Bradford Fitzgerald's place. To Bradlee's surprise, one of them was Jeremy Willows. He swept Crystal into his arms and the two of them disappeared into the crowd.

For a moment, Bradlee toyed with the idea of following her father and uncle to see what they were up to, but just then, she saw David.

He strode across the ballroom toward her, and as his gaze met hers, Bradlee's knees grew weak. She forgot all about Iris and Edward, Pamela and Jeremy, her father and uncle. She forgot the doubts and suspicions she'd been harboring for days.

But most of all, she forgot about a woman named Rachel.

He looked so handsome in his tuxedo. So worldly. It made Bradlee suddenly realize that David Powers was a fascinating man in his own right. She would have been attracted to him even if he wasn't Adam Kingsley.

"I was wondering when you'd come down." His gaze swept over her in a way that made Bradlee grow even weaker. "I've been waiting for you."

"You have?" Her voice sounded breathless. Hopeful.

He smiled down at her. "Of course. This is our big night, isn't it?"

"It's *your* big night," Bradlee replied. "Tonight you officially become Adam Kingsley."

The smile disappeared and his eyes darkened.

"Tonight won't change who I am. I haven't been Adam Kingsley in over thirty years. I don't even know who he is."

"I do," Bradlee said softly. "I've always known you."

The shadow in his eyes deepened. He started to say something, then changed his mind and took her hand instead. "Let's dance."

He pulled her onto the dance floor, and before Bradlee had time to catch her breath, she felt his strong arms close around her. For the first time all evening, she began to relax.

This was natural, she thought with an inward sigh. This was right. She and Adam together again after all those lost and lonely years.

But while Bradlee relaxed, David seemed to tense. He said against her ear, "Is it my imagination, or is everyone staring at us?"

Bradlee glanced around. It did seem as though she and David were creating something of a sensation. All eyes were on them—Iris's cool and assessing, Pamela's cold with contempt, her uncle's and her father's openly disapproving.

Bradlee shivered in David's arms, and he drew her even tighter. "I don't think Iris's announcement will come as much of a surprise to anyone," he said. "I think everyone here already knows who I am."

"You're probably right," Bradlee said. "The papers have been reporting for days now about Adam Kingsley's return. They just haven't been able to figure out your other identity."

He grimaced. "You make me sound like Clark Kent."

Bradlee laughed. "I guess in a way you are. Just think of it. How many people do you know with secret identities?"

"You might be surprised," he said dryly. "Anyway, as soon as Iris makes her announcement, the whole world will know that Adam Kingsley and David Powers are one and the same."

"And then you'll be famous. Every reporter and talk-show host in the country will be clamoring for your story."

"God, I hope not."

"You *are* going to be famous, David. At least for a while. You do realize that," Bradlee said, staring up at him.

His mouth thinned with displeasure. "Sometimes I wonder if I did the right thing, coming here." His gaze met hers and deepened. "But if I hadn't, I never would have met you."

Bradlee's heart quickened. Tingles ran up and down her spine where his hand touched her bare back. "Yes, you would have. We were destined to find each other again. I truly believe that."

Their gazes held for the longest moment, and Bradlee wondered fleetingly if she'd gone too far. Revealed too much of herself. David stopped dancing and took her hand. "Come on. Let's get out of this goldfish bowl for a while."

He led her through the open French doors onto the terrace and then down the steps to the garden. Bradlee's shoulder touched a rose and fragrant white petals floated to the ground. Lacy clouds scrolled across the moon, deepening the shadows, and even though the rain was still an hour or so away, the air was sultry and heavy with moisture. In the distance, music drifted through the open terrace doors.

David stopped at the edge of the garden. The trees were thicker here, and the night suddenly grew a little darker and quieter. A little more frightening.

He stared down at her in the moonlight. Bradlee's heart started to pound at his nearness.

"Bradlee, we have to talk."

"About what?"

"About us. About...this..." His voice trailed away as he wove his fingers through her hair and tilted her face upward while his mouth descended on hers.

Bradlee closed her eyes as his lips teased hers open, and he deepened the kiss with his tongue. His hands slipped from her hair to trace a fiery path over the contours of her body—her hips, her waist, the sides of her breasts. He touched her everywhere, and everywhere he touched, Bradlee melted. This was no ordinary kiss. This was a prelude to something wonderful.

She pressed herself to him, letting him know she was more than ready for that something.

When he finally broke the kiss, Bradlee could only gaze up at him. "David," she whispered, shaken by the power of his touch. "I like the way you communicate."

He laughed softly, still holding her in his arms. "We still have to talk."

"Yes," she agreed, standing on tiptoe to wrap her arms around his neck. "Let's talk."

This time, it was she who brought her lips to his, she who coaxed his mouth open, she who tangled her tongue with his. But David didn't resist. Far from it. He cupped her bottom with his hands, molding her body even more tightly against his and moving against her in a way so sensuous, Bradlee's every nerve-ending exploded with passion.

One kiss led to another. And then another until Bradlee lost all sense of time. All sense of reason. The only thing that mattered was David kissing her, holding her, wanting her.

His mouth trailed kisses across her cheek and down her neck, then nibbled at her ear. "Did I happen to mention how beautiful you look tonight?" he murmured.

"As a matter of fact, no," Bradlee said, reveling in his attention. In the wonder of it all.

Could this really be happening, or was she dreaming?

He drew back to gaze deeply into her eyes. "I think you're the most desirable woman I've ever known."

Bradlee melted all over again. "You make me feel that way," she whispered. "I wish we could stay out here like this forever."

Even in the moonlight, she could see a shadow in

his eyes, a darkness that made her shiver. "Bradlee—"

"I know." They weren't quite as alone in the garden as she would have wished. A third person had suddenly joined them. A woman named Rachel.

Bradlee sighed.

David reached to tuck an errant strand of hair behind her ear. "It's not as if Rachel and I are married or anything, but I *have* made a commitment to her. I do owe her my faithfulness."

"I know you do." Bradlee stared up at him in the darkness. His face looked at once familiar and mysterious to her. At once close and so very far away. "I admire you for that."

He paused, then after a moment said, "This thing between you and me...I don't know what it is. I'm not a romantic like you are. I don't believe in destiny. I'm not even sure I believe in love."

"Why not?"

He shrugged. "I guess I've never experienced it. The woman who claimed to be my mother loved me, in her own way, but she lied to me. She took me away from my family and hid the truth about my real identity. Is that love?" His tone took on a bitter edge. "Someone in my own family may have paid to have me kidnapped, and even if they didn't, no one here has exactly welcomed me home with open arms. Is *that* love?" He shrugged again. "I don't know. If it is, I'm not sure I want any part of it."

"What about you and Rachel?" Bradlee asked

quietly, wondering if she really wanted to hear his answer.

"Rachel and I have what you'd call an understanding. We suit each other. Love doesn't enter into it. As I said before, I'm not even sure I believe in love."

He lifted his head to stare at the brilliantly-lit mansion, and in the darkness, his profile was hardly more than a silhouette. Bradlee said softly, "Why is it I get the feeling you're trying to tell me something?"

He hesitated. "I don't want to hurt you. That's the last thing I want." He turned back to her and placed his hands on her shoulders. A thrill of excitement shot through her. "But I'm not sure I can be what you want me to be. I may not be the person you think I am. We had a bond when we were children, but we've been apart for over thirty years. You don't really know me, Bradlee. I'm not Adam Kingsley anymore."

"So you keep saying."

His tone sounded ironic. "I just want your eyes to be wide-open about this thing. About us."

Her heart skipped a beat. "*Is* there an us?"

He cupped his hand around the back of her neck and drew her to him, until his chin rested in her hair. "I want you. More than any woman I've ever known. I think about you all day. I dream about you at night. I can't seem to get you out of my head. I don't know—is that love?"

She expelled a shaky breath. "It'll do," she whispered. "Believe me, it'll do."

She kissed him then, with an intensity that stole

his breath away. David wrapped his arms around her, holding her close, never wanting to let her go. He'd never felt this way with Rachel—with any woman— and it was a little disconcerting for him to realize how quickly Bradlee could make him forget his commitments, his past and his future. All he wanted to think about was now, this moment, with Bradlee in his arms and the night electric with their passion.

He could have her, he knew. Bradlee was not a woman of subtleties. She didn't try to hide her true feelings. She didn't believe in game playing, and because of that, David knew he had to be honest with her. He had to make sure she understood that he wasn't promising her "tomorrow," let alone "forever." How could he commit himself to a woman like Bradlee when he didn't even know who he was anymore?

This time it was she who ended the kiss just as she had initiated it. When David would have pulled her back to him, a cooler head prevailed. "We'd better get back," he said.

"I suppose we should," she agreed.

But at the edge of the terrace, she hung back. He turned to stare down at her. Her eyes were soft and warm in the moonlight, dark pools of endless emotion. How was it he had never noticed how beautiful she was until now?

She smiled wistfully. "Fairy tales do happen, you know."

He touched her fingertips to his lips. "Tonight, you can almost make me believe that."

Chapter Twelve

A hush fell over the ballroom as Bradlee and David stepped through the doorway. The orchestra had stopped playing, and Iris stood, beckoning David to her side.

"The moment of truth," he said against Bradlee's ear. "Meet me when this is over."

She looked up at him in surprise. "Where?"

He hesitated, then said, "The nursery. I'm going to ask Iris for the key. I think it's time we face your nightmare together, Bradlee."

Before she could respond, he left her near the French doors and took his place beside Iris. Edward joined them, and Pamela moved to her husband's side, followed more reluctantly by Jeremy.

Iris's gaze swept the crowd, lingering for a brief instant on each and every face. A murmur drifted through the gathering, but when she began to speak, the silence was instant.

"You have all probably read in the papers recently that my grandson, who was kidnapped from this very house thirty-two years ago and whom we thought dead for most of those years, has finally been found. But what you don't know is that during all those years when he was dead to us, Adam knew nothing about his real family. The woman who helped Raymond Colter abduct him managed to convince him that she was his real mother and that his name was David Powers. According to David, she gave him a good home, treated him as if he were her real son. For that I'm truly grateful, even though I have not been able to bring myself to forgive her for what she did to my family. But tonight we put all that behind us to celebrate Adam's homecoming. Tonight is a night our family has waited for for over thirty years."

She reached for David's hand, and when their fingers were linked, she drew him to her side. Her blue eyes sparkled with unshed tears, and Bradlee thought she had never seen Iris so moved.

Bradlee blinked back her own tears. In spite of everything they'd been through, in spite of the fact that among the well-wishers was probably someone who had masterminded David's kidnapping, the moment was rich and poignant. After all those years, Adam Kingsley was home where he belonged.

Across the room, his gaze met Bradlee's. She couldn't tell from his expression what he was thinking, but he allowed Iris to cling to him and accepted an awkward hug from Edward. A buzz of excitement soon filled the room, and before Bradlee knew what was happening, a crowd had surrounded David, cutting him off from her view.

After a while, Bradlee saw Iris leave the ballroom on Edward's arm. He escorted her up the stairs, where Illiana waited to help her to bed.

Bradlee didn't see David anywhere. She wondered if he'd already gone up to the nursery to wait for her. Had Iris given him the key? she wondered.

Slipping from the ballroom, Bradlee made her way down the long corridor to the entrance hall and the curving front staircase. She could have used the one in the ballroom, but then someone might have seen her and questioned her departure. Or worse, followed her.

But she encountered no one on the front stairs or in the maze of hallways leading to the nursery. One of the double doors was ajar when she arrived, and Bradlee thought that David must somehow have left the ballroom without her noticing and gotten here first.

She started to call out his name, but then paused with her hand on the handle of the door. What if it wasn't David inside that room?

A shiver raced up her spine. Maybe whoever had been in the nursery with a flashlight the other night was in there again tonight. Or maybe that person had left the door unlocked. Maybe the nursery was empty.

Bradlee stood just outside the door, listening intently to the darkness within. She could hear nothing, and with a tentative motion, pulled the door open wider.

The room was pitch-black inside. Bradlee felt for

a light switch, but when she flicked it, nothing happened. Maybe that was why someone had been using a flashlight the other night, she decided. The lights were out in here. The whole thing could have been perfectly innocent. No reason in the world for her to be frightened to go inside the nursery.

Still, she held back. It wouldn't hurt to wait for David. He would be here any minute, and he would be the first to scold her for taking unnecessary chances.

Just as she started to back out of the room, Bradlee caught a very slight movement out of the corner of her eye. Her heart jumped to her throat. Had it been her imagination, or was someone in the room?

Bradlee whirled toward the door, but as she did so, she tripped over something lying on the floor. With a grunt of pain, she landed heavily on her right hip. Almost instantly a hand closed over her face. A cloth was shoved against her mouth and nose, and before Bradlee had time to struggle, blackness overcame her.

Can't breathe! a voice screamed inside her. *Can't breathe! Can't breathe!*

Chapter Thirteen

Just as David was about to slip away from the crowd and go in search of Bradlee, someone touched his shoulder from behind and a feminine voice, deep and husky, whispered in his ear, "Surprise!"

He turned to stare in shock at Rachel Hollingsworth. Her dark hair was swept back as usual, and her sultry gray eyes sparkled with excitement. She wore a strapless red gown that would and did turn heads, and as David stared down at her, she laughed delightedly.

"Well, say *something*," she urged. "Tell me how glad you are to see me. Or how much you love my dress. Or better yet—" her voice lowered seductively "—tell me how much you'd like to rip it off me."

"How did you find me?" David said instead.

Displeasure flashed in her eyes. "Is that the best you can do?" She reached up to wrap her slender arms around his neck. "Isn't it enough that I'm here?"

He removed her arms from around his neck, leading her toward the open French doors. When they were on the terrace, he let go of her arm. "Tell me how you knew about me. My name hasn't been released to the media yet. At least, it wasn't until tonight."

She laughed excitedly. "Oh, David, I can't believe this. Any of it. *You're* Adam Kingsley. My God, think of it." She made a sweeping gesture toward the mansion behind them. "All of this will be yours someday, and to think of that dump where you grew up—"

"It wasn't a dump," he said, although for the life of him he wasn't sure why he felt the need to defend the home where he'd grown up or the woman who had raised him. But he did, and fair or not, he suddenly resented Rachel's intrusion into his life.

"Oh, don't be so defensive," she pouted. "You have to admit, there isn't a house in all of Richford, New York, that can compare to this place."

"You sound impressed," David said dryly.

"Well, of course, I am. So is Daddy. He sends his regards, by the way. He isn't holding a grudge against you anymore. He understands now, as do I, why you didn't want to join the firm. But you should have told us, David. At least you should have told me. We are still engaged, aren't we?"

"You haven't answered my question," he said. "How did you know to come here?"

"Does it matter?" she asked in exasperation.

"It might."

She actually stamped her foot. "Honestly, you can

be the most tiresome man when you get focused on something.''

"Then answer the question, and we can talk about something else.''

"Talking is not exactly what I had in mind.'' The exasperation in her tone was slowly turning to anger. "You haven't even kissed me, David, and so maybe you'd better answer *my* question.''

"Which was?''

"Are we still engaged?''

He glanced away, avoiding her stare. "Look, I didn't mean to get into this with you tonight. Hell, I didn't even know you were going to be here tonight. But since you are, I think I'd better be honest with you.''

All was silent for a moment, and then a locker-room expletive exploded from Rachel's elegant lips. "I *knew* it!'' She turned to walk away from him, then whirled around to face him again. Even in the moonlight, he could see her face had gone rigid with barely suppressed rage. "I could sense something was wrong when you called that night, and then when I got the other call, my suspicions were confirmed. How dare you make me look like a fool!''

She raised her hand to slap him, but David caught her wrist in midair. Rachel was a tall woman, and their eyes were almost on the same level as they stared at each other for a long, tense moment. Then slowly David removed his hand from her wrist, and her arm dropped to her side.

"What other phone call?'' he asked quietly.

Rachel glared at him. "I don't owe you any explanations. You're the one who has the explaining to do. You're the one who's been playing around behind my back."

"I haven't been unfaithful to you," he said, although at the moment, he had to admit the argument sounded pretty lame, even to him.

"You just wanted to be, right?" Her eyes glittered like ice chips.

David felt his own anger stir to life. Maybe he was the one in the wrong here, but being on the defensive was hell. "Are you telling me you haven't been out with anyone else since I've been gone? And I'm not talking about clients."

She paused uncertainly. "I don't know what you mean."

He raised a brow at that. "Don't you? I haven't been completely cut off here, you know. I still keep in touch with the office."

In the filtered light from the terrace, David could see the telltale look of guilt flash across Rachel's features before she could subdue it. He'd only been guessing, but he knew her well enough to assume she wouldn't have been spending her evenings alone, pining for him.

She tossed back her head. "So what if I have been seeing someone? Can you honestly say you care?"

He shrugged. "It does tell me something about our relationship."

"Don't pretend you've grown sentimental all of a sudden. Look." Her voice softened, and she reached out to caress his sleeve with a smooth, slender hand. "Maybe we were never in love, but we had something better. Chemistry, David. Don't tell me you've forgotten how great it was between us." Her voice had lowered seductively again, her anger apparently vanquished. She wrapped her arms around his neck and brought her lips against his.

For a moment, David tried to respond. They were still engaged, after all, and he must have felt something for her at one time—the "chemistry" she talked about.

But if it had ever existed it was gone now, and Rachel's kiss left him cold. As cold as the woman herself. How could he ever have thought he would be happy married to her?

Because you hadn't met Bradlee, a little voice whispered inside him.

Now *there* was chemistry. But with Bradlee it was more than just passion. She was the kind of woman a man wanted to protect and cherish. She brought out qualities in David he hadn't even known he possessed.

Was that love? He thought it just might be.

He didn't resist Rachel's kiss, but neither did he respond, and after a moment, she drew back. "So I guess that's my answer, isn't it?"

She took off her engagement ring and held it out to him in her palm. The diamond sparkled coldly in the moonlight.

David wasn't sure what to do. He didn't want the ring, but he didn't think Rachel would have a use for it, either. She wasn't the sentimental type and she certainly didn't need the money.

But before he could decide how to handle the situation tactfully, her fingers closed around the diamond. She slanted a look up at him and smiled. "Did you think it would be that easy, David?"

"I don't want to hurt you, Rachel, but it's over. Don't make it harder than it has to be."

She laughed then—a dark, humorless laugh that filled David with dread. "Did you think I would just go quietly back to New York and forget all about...you?"

He could have sworn what she meant to say was "this." "Forget all about this." While he had no illusions about her undying devotion to him, he could see where his newfound identity—and all that went with it—would make it harder for a woman like Rachel to let go.

But then, maybe he was being too hard on her. Trying to justify his actions and assuage his own guilty conscience by making her seem cold and mercenary. What did that say about his own character? he wondered.

"I'm sure the Kingsleys won't mind you staying the night," he said. "But in the morning, I think it would be best if you went back to New York. In a few days, I'll fly up and we can talk some more if you like."

She lifted her chin, eyeing him with cold amusement. "Don't worry about me, David. Your grandmother has issued me a standing invitation. I can stay as long as I want, but I wouldn't dream of cramping your style. Besides, I've already made other friends in Memphis.''

She started to pass by him, but David caught her arm. ''What other friends? What was the phone call you mentioned earlier?''

She brushed his hand off her arm and smiled. ''You have your secrets, and I have mine.''

BRADLEE AWAKENED WITH a splitting headache, and for a moment, she had to lie perfectly still to keep from blacking out again. A medicinal odor lingered in the air, a scent that was sickeningly sweet and vaguely familiar. A memory reached out to her, something that had come back to her while under hypnosis.

She had smelled the same scent the night of the kidnapping. The shadow had bent over Adam's bed, holding something to his face. Bradlee had been worried that he couldn't breathe, that someone was trying to smother him, but now she knew what had happened. Whoever had come into the nursery had held ether to David's face to ensure he wouldn't wake up for hours, not until he and the kidnapper were long gone.

She struggled to her feet. Her head spun dizzily but she knew she had little time to waste. Whoever had knocked her out would be back, and in her weakened condition, Bradlee might not be able to defend herself—especially against any kind of weapon.

The room was dark. The blinds were all drawn,

shutting out the moonlight, and she knew the light switch was useless. With her arms outstretched, Bradlee slowly crossed the room until her hands touched a solid surface. She felt along the wall until she reached the door, then fumbled for the handle. Once again, the room had been locked from the outside.

Trying to swallow her panic, Bradlee tried the handle a second time. She beat on the door, calling out for help, but she knew that, too, was useless. The nursery was located in a wing of the house far away from the ballroom. No one would be around unless it was David.

Or the kidnapper...

Bradlee turned, feeling her way in the darkness. There was another door, wasn't there? One that led into the nanny's room.

A little more frantically now, Bradlee slid her hands along the wall, searching for the door. Just when she was about to give up, she felt the sharp edges of the door frame. But here again, the knob wouldn't yield. She shook it repeatedly, then beat on the door.

Telling herself not to panic, Bradlee turned and leaned her back against the door, letting herself slide to the floor.

And that was when she saw her way out. A sliver of light, invisible when she'd been standing, showed beneath the blinds at the bottom of the French doors to the balcony. Those doors would surely be bolted from the inside. If she could get them open, she could

stand on the balcony and shout for help until someone in the gardens heard her.

Crossing the room hurriedly, she banged her shin
against a bed and stubbed her toe on a rocking chair
as she made her way to the light. Panic bubbled inside her again as another thought occurred to her.
What if the French doors were locked from the inside
with a key rather than a bolt? She would still be
trapped.

I'll break a window, she thought, and immediately
the panic subsided.

*See? There's a way out. You just have to remain
calm and think.*

"Okay," she whispered. "I'm calm. I'm thinking." And to her relief, the bolt on the doors turned
easily. Pulling one of the doors open, she stepped out
onto the balcony.

It had started to rain, and dark clouds blocked the
moon. The gardens below lay in shadow, and because of the rain, no one was about. Everyone had
gone back inside. The outside doors of the ballroom
had undoubtedly been closed to the weather. Bradlee
could stand out here and shout all night, and no one
would hear her.

She shivered in the rain, wondering what to do
now. She couldn't stay here indefinitely. For all she
knew, whoever had attacked her would be coming
back for her. With the doors all locked in the nursery,
the only way out was down.

She leaned over the railing and heard a cracking
sound. The whole length of the coping moved under

her weight, and Bradlee stepped back, wondering how long it had been since anyone had actually stood on this balcony. The floor seemed sound enough, but the railing was definitely unsteady.

Bradlee moved first to one end of the balcony and then the other, searching for a means of escape. A rose trellis clung to the brick wall of the house about two feet over from one corner of the balcony and perhaps four feet down. In order to reach it, she would have to climb over the balcony, hang from the railing with one hand while reaching with the other for the trellis.

If she missed…if she fell…a stone terrace waited for her thirty feet below.

She might not be killed, Bradlee reasoned as she put a leg over the balcony railing; just every bone in her body broken.

"That's it, think positively," she muttered. The rain was still light, but it was enough to make the balcony dangerously slippery. Both legs were over the railing now, and she clung to the edge as she inched herself as close to the wall as she could get. Glancing down, she spotted the trellis below her. She could touch it with her foot, but in order to grab hold, she would have to let go of the railing.

Squatting, she let her hands slide down two of the railing posts. Then, clinging with one hand, she reached for the trellis. The coping shifted beneath her weight, and Bradlee felt herself slipping. She grabbed for the railing post again, but in horror, she felt it rip loose from the rest of the coping. Acting purely on instinct, Bradlee lunged for the trellis.

Rose thorns bit into her skin as she scrambled for purchase. For a split second, she thought she was going to be all right, and then the trellis slats began to snap loose from their frame.

She fell a good five feet before she managed to grab hold of the trellis again. Clinging to wood and vines, thorns tearing at her skin, Bradlee held her breath. Her heartbeat roared in her ears, and her arms and legs were shaking. But the trellis held.

After a few minutes, she began to climb down. It felt like an eternity before she reached the ground, and by the time she did, her dress was in tatters and her hands and arms were bleeding from dozens of scratches.

She drew a long breath that turned into a sob, but she wouldn't let herself give in to her terror. Not yet. Keeping to the deepest shadows of the garden, she ran around to the rear entrance. The house was ominously silent, and glancing at her watch, Bradlee realized why. She'd been out for longer than she'd thought. The party was over.

Feeling disoriented, she slipped through the pantries and huge kitchen, then made her way up the back stairs and headed down the long hallway to her room. Once inside, she closed and locked her door, leaning against the heavy wood as she shut her eyes and tried to calm her racing heart.

Only then did she let herself think about how close a call she'd just had. Only then did she let herself wonder who might have knocked her out and locked her in the nursery. And for what purpose.

David was the only one who knew she would be there, but someone could have overheard them talking or followed her. Bradlee had no way of knowing who, but David had been right about one thing: The party had drawn out Colter's accomplice. And he— or she—was even more desperate than they'd realized. And more dangerous.

Her arms and hands stinging like wildfire, Bradlee crossed the room to the bathroom, shedding her ruined dress and torn stockings as she went. Standing in her underwear in front of the sink, she washed the scratches with warm, soapy water, gritting her teeth against the pain. She found antiseptic in the medicine cabinet and sprayed every single cut, crying out at the stinging hurt.

What to do now? she wondered, walking back into the bedroom as she blew on her hands and arms. Call the police? And tell them what? Again she had no proof, except the broken railing on the balcony and the scratches on her hands and arms. But she hadn't seen her attacker. She couldn't give a description. So what purpose would be served by bringing in the police—except, perhaps, to make herself look like a fool?

What she needed to do now was talk to David. She wasn't exactly thinking straight at the moment, and a cooler head was needed. David would know what to do.

Drawing on jeans and a T-shirt, Bradlee unlocked

her door and peered into the hallway. No one was about. She was just about to let herself out, when David's door opened and a woman walked out.

Shocked, Bradlee quickly stepped behind her own door, but left it open enough so that she could see down the hallway. The woman was tall, dark, and exotically beautiful, the most gorgeous creature Bradlee had ever seen. But what made her even more striking was the white lace negligee she wore. Even in the dim light of the hallway, her lithe body was silhouetted beneath the filmy fabric, leaving nothing to the imagination.

Bradlee knew who she was immediately. The intimate way she turned her head and smiled back into the room could only mean one thing. Rachel Hollingsworth, David's fiancée, had been invited to the party and had shown up late. That was why David hadn't come up to the nursery as planned.

Bradlee felt a sick sensation in the pit of her stomach. There was no way she could compete with Rachel Hollingsworth. Bradlee had worked with beautiful models most of her adult life, and had never felt particularly intimidated. She'd never had any illusions about on her own appearance, had accepted long ago that she had the kind of girl-next-door looks that were pleasant enough but would never stop traffic.

Rachel Hollingsworth would not only stop traffic, she would create a monumental traffic jam.

In a moment, David appeared in the doorway. He still wore his tuxedo pants, but he'd removed his jacket and his white shirt was unbuttoned. It took little imagination to figure out that a reunion had been taking place in his room. In spite of what he'd said earlier, Bradlee didn't think he'd been *talking* to Rachel.

They were talking now, though, murmuring in such low tones that Bradlee couldn't hear what they were saying. Not wanting to be caught eavesdropping, she eased her bedroom door closed and walked across the room to her bed. Sitting down on the edge, she felt frustrated tears pool in her eyes.

She could have been killed tonight while David had been enjoying an intimate little reunion with his fiancée. No matter what he'd said earlier about talking with Rachel, Bradlee didn't think it would be that easy to break it off with a woman like her. What man would be able to resist her?

Falling back on the bed, she held up her hands, examining the angry red scratches. While she'd been climbing down the trellis, David had been holding Rachel in his arms, kissing her as he'd kissed Bradlee earlier. But he wouldn't have had to stop with Rachel. He didn't owe Bradlee his fidelity. He didn't owe her anything. They were hardly more than strangers, really—two people who'd been brought back together because of an old tragedy.

A tragedy that had affected both their lives; but that was all their relationship was. In fairness, David had tried to tell her that. He'd warned her that he didn't believe in destiny.

Why hadn't she listened? Why had she continued to pursue a dream that had eluded her all her life?

Chapter Fourteen

Bradlee was just finishing breakfast on the terrace the next morning when David came down to join her. She looked around, expecting to see Rachel, but then assumed she was probably sleeping in. She'd had a late night, after all.

Bradlee tried to ignore David when he sat down beside her, but he angled his head, forcing her to look at him. "Good morning," he said, and Bradlee wanted to slug him.

Instead she glanced at him coolly. "Good morning."

"Where did you disappear to last night?" he asked. "I looked all over for you."

Bradlee cut him a glance. "You're kidding, right?"

He frowned. "Why would I kid about that?"

She tossed down her napkin and got up. "For your information, I was in the nursery last night. Where were you?"

"I thought you might have gone up without me,

so I went to check. But when I got there, the door was locked. You weren't there.''

Bradlee lifted one brow. "Oh, I was there, all right. But it's a long story, and I'm sure you have more important things to do.''

She had the satisfaction of seeing his puzzled expression before she whirled and strode down the terrace steps. He caught up with her and grabbed her arm. Bradlee half turned and gave him a quelling look. "Let go of me, please.''

"What's the matter with you?''

She glanced at his hand still on her arm, then lifted her gaze to meet his. "If you must know, someone tried to kill me last night while you were with *her*.''

His grip tightened on her arm. "Bradlee, what happened? What are you talking about?''

"Oh, I'm not blaming you," she said, trying to control her anger. "Why shouldn't you be with her? You're engaged, after all. But we did agree to meet at the nursery, remember?''

"I remember, and I was there. I didn't think you were. And Bradlee—" She started to walk away but he pulled her back. "I'm not engaged anymore.''

That stopped her. It was her turn to be shocked. She stared up at him. "You're...not?''

He shook his head. "I'll tell you all about it, but first, tell me what happened last night. You said someone tried to kill you—" For the first time, he noticed the deep scratches on her arms. He lifted her hands gently, examined the marks, then slowly met her gaze. "My God, what happened? Who the hell did this to you?"

The anger in his eyes was perhaps the most gratifying emotion Bradlee had ever witnessed. It was a primal, masculine reaction that stirred something feminine inside her. She almost smiled. "You really aren't engaged anymore?"

He scowled down at her, his anger momentarily directed at her. "No, but for God's sake, don't change the subject. I need to know what happened to you last night. Who's responsible for this?" He was still holding her hands, as if they were his private property, his most treasured possessions.

Bradlee felt a rush of excitement as she gazed up at him. "Actually, I did that myself," she said. "Climbing down the rose trellis by the nursery." Then she went on to explain everything that had happened to her the evening before. When she finished, David's expression was like a thundercloud—dark, menacing, and possibly deadly.

"Someone must have overheard me asking Iris for the key last night," he said. "She knew we both wanted to look around in the room, and she told me she would leave the key on a table in her sitting room when she went up for the night. But when I got up there, I couldn't find the key, and Illiana said that Iris had already gone to bed and didn't want to be disturbed. Someone must have gotten there before me and taken the key without Iris or Illiana knowing about it. Then whoever it was went up to the nursery to wait for you."

Bradlee shivered. "Someone's getting desperate, David. We're getting too close to the truth."

"We'd better get up to the nursery and take a look around," he said grimly. "Whoever knocked you out may have left a clue, and if so, I want to find it before he has time to cover his tracks."

"He?"

David shrugged. "Or she. I'm going up to see Iris now and find out about that key. Don't go anywhere near the nursery until I get back."

"Don't worry," Bradlee assured him. "I always try to learn from my mistakes."

AFTER DAVID LEFT, Bradlee walked around the garden for a few minutes before returning to the terrace. She knew she should try to concentrate on remembering who had been in the nursery on the night of the kidnapping, but all she could think about was David's broken engagement.

She didn't want to take pleasure in someone else's misfortune, but she couldn't honestly say she was sorry. Something special had happened between her and David, and it would have killed her to see him marry someone else. They were meant to be together. For Bradlee, it was as simple as that.

When she walked back into the house, she saw Rachel Hollingsworth descending the stairs. One of the servants trailed behind her, carrying her luggage. Bradlee wasn't sure if she should stop and introduce herself, or pretend she didn't know who Rachel was.

Instead, as they met at the foot of the stairs, Bradlee nodded and smiled, and then started up.

Rachel Hollingsworth said coolly, "So you're Bradlee."

She turned in surprise. "Yes. And you must be Rachel."

One dark brow arched elegantly. "So you've heard about me. From David, no doubt."

Bradlee paused, not wanting a scene, but sensing Rachel was spoiling for one. In a verbal sparring match, Rachel Hollingsworth would probably be unsurpassed.

And this morning, she would also be looking for someone to blame. Had David told her about Bradlee? And if he had, what, exactly, had he said?

Rachel glanced over her shoulder at the man carrying her luggage. "Take my bags outside and put them in the car. I'll be there shortly."

The man inclined his head and did as he was told. Rachel turned back to Bradlee. "You think you've got him, don't you? I wouldn't celebrate just yet if I were you. David and I are very well suited to one another. We're both ambitious, intelligent, and we know how to go after what we want. In spite of what you think, you're not the right woman for him."

"Don't you think he should be the judge of that?"

Rachel leaned toward her, and Bradlee fought the urge to step back. The woman reminded her of a cat—sleek, well-groomed, with razor-sharp claws just out of sight.

"You think you have some kind of hold on him

because of the past. Oh, yes,'' she said, when Bradlee looked at her in surprise. "I know all about the kidnapping, the fact that you were in the nursery with him when he was taken. In fact, I know quite a lot about you."

Bradlee suppressed a shudder. The woman was like *ice*. How had David ever fallen for someone like her? "How do you know so much about me?"

Rachel smiled. "I don't think I want you to know that. At least, not yet." She turned, but at the door she stopped and looked over her shoulder. "For your information—and David's—I won't be returning to New York. I've decided to stay in Memphis for a while."

"Why?" Bradlee asked her flatly.

Rachel smiled again. "I've made some very good friends here."

IRIS WAS STILL IN BED that morning, recovering from the excitement of the night before. She reclined against a stack of pillows, her white hair smoothed back from her face, highlighting the deep wrinkles that David had never noticed before. She wore no makeup, and for the first time since he'd met her, she looked her age. Gone was the regal air, the arrogant demeanor. Today she looked like a frail, old woman who couldn't quite muster the strength to get out of bed.

To David's surprise, she reached for his hand when he came to stand by her bedside. Her skin felt like parchment, dry and almost unbearably fragile.

Last night she'd appeared to be a woman who could live forever, but David realized it had only been an act. And the performance had taken its toll. He wondered how much longer his grandmother had left, and it hit him suddenly that, under different circumstances, she might have been someone he would have enjoyed knowing.

"Sit down, David," she murmured and released his hand to pat the edge of her bed. He did as he was told, and she smiled. "Tell me. Did you enjoy last night? Was it everything you expected it to be?"

"I didn't find out who helped Raymond Colter kidnap me, if that's what you mean," he said. "But it was an interesting evening, nonetheless."

She looked amused. "Your fiancée is a very beautiful woman. You should have told me about her. I would have sent her a personal invitation."

David stared down at her. "Didn't you?"

"How could I? I knew nothing about her."

David wasn't sure if he believed her or not. Iris, like Rachel, was a woman of secrets. Neither one of them was as open as Bradlee, and rather than finding their guile appealing, David found it disturbing. They were both capable of manipulation, and there wasn't a man alive who didn't resent that. David was no exception.

He shrugged. "I didn't invite her, either. I'm wondering how she found out about all this."

"Does it matter?" Iris inquired mildly.

"That's exactly what she asked."

"Let me put it another way," Iris said. "Would it

have mattered if her timing had not been so inopportune?''

''Meaning?''

Iris gave him a knowing look. ''Meaning Bradlee. You've fallen in love with her, haven't you?''

David glanced at her, startled.

She chuckled. ''You're so like your grandfather. Refusing to believe what's staring you in the face. Bradlee's a wonderful girl. She's always had a... fascination for you.''

The hesitation before the word made David wonder what she had meant to say instead. Suddenly, he didn't want to talk about Bradlee to Iris. It was a protective instinct he didn't quite understand.

''I came up here to ask you about the key to the nursery,'' he said, deliberately changing the subject. ''You said you would leave it for me in your sitting room last night.''

''And I did,'' Iris replied. ''I put it on the table exactly where I said I would.''

''When I came up, it wasn't there,'' David told her. ''Illiana told me you'd already gone to bed and didn't want to be disturbed, so I left. I went up to the nursery to meet Bradlee, but the door was locked and she wasn't there. This morning she told me when she got to the nursery, the door was open. She went in and someone used ether to knock her out.''

Iris sat up in alarm. ''My God. Is she all right?''

''Other than several scratches, she's fine.''

''Scratches?''

"She was locked in the nursery, and the only way she could get out was to climb down the rose trellis."

Iris had gone completely white. She lay back against the pillows, her hand at her heart. "My God, she could have been killed. Why would someone do such a thing?"

"Because Bradlee was in the nursery the night I was kidnapped. Someone is obviously afraid that she saw something, and now that I've come back, she might remember."

"No." The word was barely audible, but Iris's eyes were shadowed with an emotion David could only call fear. "I refuse to believe someone in this house had anything to do with your kidnapping. Your own family, for God's sake."

"I'm not saying it's someone in this family. It could have been someone at the party last night. That's why I wanted to invite the same people here, but I certainly didn't mean to put Bradlee's life in danger."

Iris lifted her hand as if to gesture, but then dropped it weakly to the bed. She shook her head almost imperceptibly. "I cannot stand to think about this."

"Then don't," David said, alarmed by her pallor. Maybe he shouldn't have told her about Bradlee's attack. Iris had already been in a weakened state, and he should have been more sensitive. "There's no need for you to worry about any of this." Impulsively he took her hand and held it for a brief moment. "I'll take care of everything. But I'm afraid I still need a key to the nursery. I have to go up and take a look around.''

Iris nodded. ''You haven't called the police, have you? The publicity...''

''Not yet,'' David said grimly. ''But I may have to. My main concern at this point is Bradlee's safety. I don't care about the publicity.''

''But you must,'' Iris said in a feeble voice, ''now that you're a Kingsley.''

AT IRIS'S DIRECTION, Illiana managed to produce another key for David, and a few minutes later, he opened the door of the nursery and entered. Bradlee followed him inside, and for the longest moment, neither of them spoke a word. They stood in the center of the room, gazing around.

''Try not to touch anything,'' he said. ''We don't want to disturb any evidence.''

The blinds were still drawn, and the gloom added to the ominous atmosphere. Bradlee had left the French door open the night before, and a draft gave the room the chill of a tomb. The hair on the back of her neck rose up, but Bradlee thought the feeling had more to do with what had happened in the room thirty-two years ago than with her experience last night.

One tiny bed remained in the nursery. The other two—Andrew's and the one Bradlee had slept in that night—had been removed, but Adam's bed had been left untouched all these years, waiting for his return.

She glanced at David. He was staring down at the

bed, too, and for a moment, he seemed to have forgotten her presence. Then he roused himself. ''Remember anything?''

''Not yet.'' She took a deep breath, gazing around. She pointed to the door across the room. ''That door leads to the nanny's room. It was locked last night.''

David crossed the room and taking a handkerchief from his pocket, tried the door. ''We'll probably have to unlock it from the hallway if we want to have a look around.''

''I don't really think there's a need to,'' Bradlee said softly. ''This is where it happened.'' And they both knew she was once again talking about the past.

David walked over to the balcony. He stepped outside and after a moment, he called her name. Bradlee reluctantly joined him. Last night she hadn't had time to consider that Adam's kidnapper had gained access to the nursery in the very way that she had escaped, but now the irony was chilling.

David's expression was grave when he turned to face her. ''It's a wonder you weren't killed. Look.'' She came uneasily to stand beside him. He was staring down at the missing post from the balcony railing, the one that had come loose in her hand the night before.

She shivered. ''It's falling apart. I found that out last night. No one's likely been out here for years. I'm not so sure we should be standing here.''

''The balcony itself is solid enough.'' Something in his tone made Bradlee's heart start to beat in slow, painful jerks. He straightened to stare at her. "But the railing has been pried loose."

Her heart slammed against her chest then. "You're saying last night was all some kind of setup? I was *meant* to fall off the balcony?"

"You were locked in the nursery with only one way out. And that way was booby-trapped."

Bradlee was shaking. She wrapped her arms around her middle. "I'm not so sure we can handle this alone anymore, David. I think it's time we call the police."

He knelt to examine the railing again. "I'm thinking the same thing. We probably should have reported the Dr. Scott episode, but it's too late to worry about that now." He stood and took her arm. "Come on. Let's go make the call."

IRIS WAS FURIOUS. All through the interview with Sergeant Packer, it was obvious she was seething. Having the police called in behind her back was tantamount to treason, and she was not likely to let Bradlee and David forget it.

Immediately after Sergeant Packer departed, Iris rose without a word and had Illiana help her upstairs and back into bed. Once she was out of earshot, Pamela's own carefully controlled demeanor cracked. She turned on Bradlee and David in a fury. "How dare you make fools of all of us like that? Have you any idea what you've done? When the media get wind of this, we'll be swarmed. Our pictures will be splashed across every sleazy newspaper in the country." She got up and started to pace.

Bradlee said, "Sergeant Packer promised he'd tried to keep it as quiet as possible."

Pamela paused to give her a I-don't-believe-you look. "They always say that, don't they? Then the next thing you know, you're being hounded by reporters. You can't even go out of the house."

"Mother's right," Jeremy chimed in. "You should have consulted with the rest of us before you called in the police. Something like this affects all our lives."

"Do you think they care about that?" Pamela demanded. She turned to Bradlee and David. "You two have caused nothing but trouble since the moment you set foot in this house."

"What I can't understand," David said slowly, his gaze cool and assessing as it moved from Pamela to Jeremy, "is why no one here seems in the least concerned about what happened to Bradlee. She could have been killed."

Edward rose at that and set his drink aside. He'd remained quiet all through the interview with the police and afterward, but now he came toward Bradlee. "David's right. I'm very sorry about what happened. I can't imagine who would have done such a thing."

"We don't know that anyone did anything," Pamela said icily. "According to your father, you've always been given to flights of fantasy. Isn't it possible you imagined the whole episode?"

Bradlee held out her arms, displaying the deep red

scratches from the rose vines. "Did I imagine these, too?"

Pamela shrugged. "Oh, I've no doubt it happened much the way you described it. But isn't it possible that you panicked when you got inside the nursery? Considering what happened in the past, it would be only natural. You were very traumatized by Adam's kidnapping."

"How do you explain someone knocking me out?" Bradlee asked. "Or the locked door?"

Jeremy took up his mother's argument. "Maybe a draft from the hallway blew the door closed after you were inside and it locked automatically. Overcome with terror, you fainted. When you came to, you thought you'd been attacked. Again you panicked, and when you couldn't get the door open, you decided to climb down the trellis."

Obviously, he and Pamela had discussed this scenario previously.

David said, "That doesn't explain how the balcony railing came to be pried loose from the frame."

"No one has been out on that balcony for years," Pamela said. "The wood probably just rotted away."

"I don't think so," David said. "The railing had been tampered with."

"You're an expert on such matters, are you?" Jeremy asked coolly.

David replied just as coolly, "I've examined a few crime scenes, yes. Haven't you?"

"I'm not a criminal attorney."

"Then I guess you'll have to take my word for

it," David said. "And Sergeant Packer's. He agreed that it looked as if a portion of the railing had been deliberately separated from the frame."

"That's ridiculous," Pamela argued. "If someone wanted to get rid of Bradlee, why didn't they just kill her while she was unconscious?"

"Because they wanted it to look like an accident," David said. "They wanted everyone to jump to the same conclusion you and Jeremy just outlined so brilliantly."

For a moment, Pamela didn't seem to catch David's meaning, but Jeremy did. He took a step forward. "Now see here. If you're accusing us—"

Pamela gasped. "How dare you?"

"Oh, I dare," David retorted. "I'll dare to do and say a lot of things until I find out who tried to kill Bradlee."

Bradlee had just finished drying her hair that night when someone knocked on her bedroom door. She drew on a silk robe over her short nightgown and crossed the room to the door. "Who is it?"

"David."

She drew back the door and he strode into the room. "I've been thinking about something all evening, and I want to run it by you. What if the trap set in the nursery wasn't meant for you, after all? What if it was meant for...me...?" His words trailed off as he turned to face her for the first time. Something sparked in his eyes as his gaze lowered to the deep vee where the sides of her robe met.

Self-conscious, Bradlee pulled the robe more snugly around her. "I just got out of the shower," she mumbled.

"So did I," David said absently, his gaze still on her. He ran a hand through his damp hair, looking distracted.

Bradlee closed the door and leaned against it. "What did you mean, the trap might have been set for you? Why?"

"Why?" He was focusing on her legs now and seemed to have lost track of his thoughts. Then, with an effort, he tore his gaze away and walked over to the French doors. Opening them, he stepped out, and Bradlee followed.

"I went up and examined the railing again," he told her. "It was pulled loose from the frame about here." He demonstrated what he meant. "Just enough so that it probably wouldn't be detected. But that also meant it wasn't loose enough to come apart immediately with your weight. You were able to grab hold of the trellis and save yourself from falling. But supposing someone heavier than you, someone like me, for instance, had been the one climbing over that railing? It would have broken apart instantly. I wouldn't have had time to grab for anything but thin air."

"But I'm the one who saw something the night you were kidnapped," Bradlee said.

"Maybe it didn't have anything to do with the kidnapping."

"What do you mean?"

David shrugged. "I'm saying I think we may have overlooked a critical piece of the puzzle. Let's assume my mother was right. Someone at the fund-raiser that night paid Raymond Colter to kidnap me. Maybe you really did see that person in the nursery. But it's been over thirty years. The secret has been safe all this time. Why would my being found or your coming back here cause Colter's accomplice to panic? After all, if you couldn't finger him back then, why would he think you'd be able to now?"

"Go on," Bradlee prompted.

"When I made the announcement that I intended to find out who was behind my kidnapping, I may have laid the groundwork for an even deadlier plan. If someone were after the Kingsley fortune, I'd be the last person he'd want around. By making my death look as if it were tied to the kidnapping, the police would have a whole slew of suspects to investigate, namely, everyone who was present the night of the fund-raiser and the night of my party."

"You keep saying 'he,'" Bradlee said. "I take it you have someone in mind."

"The one person who would benefit most from my death has an airtight alibi for the night I was kidnapped," David said. "I pointed it out to him myself."

"Jeremy Willows."

David nodded. "Makes a certain amount of twisted sense when you think about it. You said yourself he's remained in this house all these years hoping to become Iris's heir. With me around, that may not happen.''

''All right, I can buy your reasoning up to a certain point,'' Bradlee said. ''But what about Dr. Scott? What about what happened to me in her office?''

''Since we didn't take you to the hospital, we can't be sure anything really happened. You could have just gotten sick, maybe from the anxiety of the hypnosis.''

Bradlee frowned. ''I'm beginning to feel as though you think I'm paranoid. First Jeremy and Pamela accuse me of imagining the episode in the nursery, and now you're suggesting I made up the scene with Dr. Scott. I suppose I never overheard her conversation on the telephone, either,'' she said peevishly.

''No, I'm sure you heard exactly what you thought you did. Dr. Scott's disappearance seems to bear that out. She may even have given you something while you were under, but that doesn't disprove my theory. Maybe Colter's accomplice did call Dr. Scott to find out if you'd remembered anything. But you hadn't. So why would he need to worry? Why risk exposure by getting rid of you when, by all indications, it isn't necessary?''

''If what you're saying is true,'' Bradlee said, ''then I'm not the one in danger. You are.''

''It's only guesswork, and the bottom line is still this. You could have been killed last night. I think it's time we consider getting you away from here.''

Bradlee glanced at him sharply. ''You don't mean

that. I can't go away now. You need me to help you find the person who paid Colter to kidnap you."

"Bradlee." He took her by the shoulders, holding her in front of him. "In case you haven't noticed, I'm not a kid anymore. I can take care of myself, and I don't want anything to happen to you."

"Nothing will," Bradlee said. "I'll be a lot more careful from now on. But David—" her voice grew soft with emotion "—I've waited over thirty years for you to come back. Don't send me away now."

His gaze deepened as he lifted his hand to her hair, tangling his fingers in the damp strands. "What am I going to do with you?"

"I can think of a few things," she said, closing her eyes briefly at the softness of his touch.

Both of his hands wove through her hair, holding her face up to his. Their eyes met for one brief, electric moment before his mouth claimed hers in a soul-shattering kiss that was anything but soft.

Bradlee pressed her body to his as his hands left her hair to skim heatedly over the silky contours of her robe.

Then his hands were between them, untying the belt, and in an instant, the robe slithered from her shoulders. He lifted her into his arms and carried her into the bedroom, not once breaking the kiss.

Bradlee had never felt so adored. So...loved. She wanted him now, instantly, more than she ever thought possible.

But David had something else in mind—a slow, silky seduction that began at her lips and ended with her toes. And then moved all the way back up again. Over and over.

In the throes of deep passion, Bradlee whispered the words she'd waited a lifetime to utter: "I love you. I love you. I love you."

Chapter Fifteen

"I love you. I love you. I love you."

The words repeated themselves in David's head as he propped himself on his elbow and watched Bradlee sleep. She looked so vulnerable, lying on her side with the covers pulled up to her chin. Her hair lay in silky waves against the pillow. He resisted the urge to touch it. He didn't want to wake her. Not yet, anyway. Not until he had some time to think things through.

"I love you. I love you. I love you."

Such an honest proclamation of her feelings...and so like Bradlee. There were no half measures with her. It was all or nothing, and she would never try to hide her emotions. She would never try to pretend that tonight meant nothing to her. But that was exactly what David intended to do.

It would hurt her, he knew, but what choice did he have?

As quietly as he could, he rose from bed and slipped on his clothes, then stood for a long moment, gazing down at her.

He couldn't allow her to put herself in danger because of him. He didn't yet know who the target was—himself or Bradlee—but the fact remained that she could have been killed last night. Or at the very least, seriously injured; and that just wasn't acceptable. David had to do whatever he could to protect her, and that meant sending her way.

She wouldn't want to go, of course. Especially not after they'd made love, but David would somehow have to convince her it was in his best interests that she return to L.A.

And, he thought grimly, there was only one way to do that.

WHEN BRADLEE AWAKENED she was alone in her bed. She sat up, reaching for her nightgown. "David?"

"Out here."

She slipped the nightgown over her head and stepped onto the balcony. "What are you doing?"

"Thinking." He was perched on the railing, staring into the darkness. When she approached him, he put an arm around her shoulders, but there was no warmth in the touch.

Bradlee shivered. "What are you thinking about?"

He glanced at her then, but she couldn't read his expression in the darkness. "About everything. Us. What happened earlier."

"Oh, no," Bradlee said, a sinking sensation in her stomach. "Don't say it. Don't you dare say it."

"What?"

"You regret it. It never should have happened. It was all a mistake."

"Bradlee, it was." His voice was gentle, but that did little to assuage the disappointment, the pain that tore through her.

She took a step back from him. "How can you say that? It was wonderful. It was—"

"Fireworks? Explosions? The earth moved?"

She hated the cynical tone in his voice. "For me, it was," she said softly.

He was silent for a moment. "Look, I'll admit it was great for me, too. But it doesn't—"

"Mean anything?" It was her turn to finish his sentence.

"Not the way you want it to." He straightened from the railing and came toward her. She could suddenly see his expression in the moonlight, and Bradlee shivered again. His eyes were dark and shuttered, not at all what she'd hoped to see.

"I told you once before, I don't believe in fairy tales and destiny and all that stuff you talk about. You've built a fantasy in your head, kept it alive all these years by hoping Adam Kingsley would someday come back and sweep you off your feet. When you look at me, you don't see the man I really am. You see the fantasy. The man you want me to be."

Bradlee shook her head. "That's not true."

"Isn't it?" His gaze hardened. "Then why did you call me Adam?"

"I didn't."

"Yes, you did. At a...shall we say...critical moment earlier you called out Adam's name."

Bradlee started to deny it again, but then she stopped. *Had* she called him Adam?

As if sensing her hesitation, he said, "Bradlee, I don't want to hurt you, but I can't give you what you want right now. I just got out of one entanglement. I don't need another."

Was that all he thought she was? An "entanglement"?

She drew her fingers through her hair. "That didn't seem to stop you earlier," she said angrily.

"No, but it should have. I can't deal with a relationship right now. There's too much happening in my life. I have to have some space."

"Meaning?" She followed him back inside the room, watched him walk toward the door.

He turned, his expression resolved. "Meaning I think you should go back to L.A. Give us some time apart. Maybe that'll put everything into perspective for you. At any rate, I'll be going back to New York in a few weeks and..." He trailed off with a shrug.

"We may as well end it now, right?" Bradlee marveled at how calm she sounded, how in control she appeared when her life was crumbling around her. She was in love with a man who didn't love her. Who didn't even want her around. What did that say about her?

"Look, it's for the best," he said at the door. "Once you get back to Los Angeles, you'll probably agree with me."

Bradlee folded her arms and glared at him. "Maybe I already do."

Something flickered in his eyes. Was it disappointment? Pain?

Wishful thinking, Bradlee told herself. Because in the next instant, he turned and walked out the door without looking back.

BRADLEE DIDN'T GO BACK to bed after David left, but sat up instead and tried to figure out what had gone wrong. She was hurt, angry, and not a little embarrassed, but she wouldn't give in to those emotions. Not just yet. What she had to do now was decide her next move.

Sometime just before dawn, she realized there was actually very little she could do. This was David's home now, and he'd asked her to leave. She'd become an unwelcome guest, and Bradlee had enough pride left not to hang around where she wasn't wanted.

She would go away quietly, with dignity, she decided. Like any good guardian angel who'd overstayed her usefulness.

THE NEXT MORNING, David decided he'd better figure out a way to avoid Bradlee while still keeping an eye on her. He couldn't be sure how much danger she was in, or whether he himself might be the target, but he knew he would breathe a lot easier once she was on a plane back to L.A. Having to witness the pain in her eyes last night was a pretty big price to pay for his own peace of mind, but no price was too high for her safety.

To her credit, she hadn't broken down last night when he'd told her he wanted her to leave. She hadn't made accusations or threats as some women would have done, nor had she ranted and raved, though he knew she'd been angry.

What she had done was agree that he could be right. Once she got away from him, she might find she was over him. Might even find there'd been nothing there to begin with.

That still smarted, David had to admit, but he couldn't blame her. He'd been deliberately cold and callous, and she'd had no way of knowing his real motive.

He walked out into the gardens, where he could see the front drive. If anyone came in, he wanted to know about it.

He'd been outside for about fifteen minutes when his cell phone rang. He flipped it open and lifted it to his ear.

"Hello?"

"Adam Kingsley?"

David frowned. "Who is this?"

"Don't you recognize my voice, boy?"

It came to him then. "Colter."

"Don't hang up. I used my weekly phone privilege to call you."

"What do you want?" David asked impatiently. He wasn't about to hang up, but he wouldn't let Colter know that.

"You still want to talk?"

"I might."

Colter paused. "Bring some cash. We'll see if we can cut a deal."

He hung up before David could query him further, but the first question that came to mind was how the hell Colter had gotten his cell-phone number.

David stared up at the mansion, thinking. It would take him hours to make the drive up to the penitentiary and back. He wouldn't be here to watch out for Bradlee until she got on a plane. Something about this whole setup didn't smell right, but then again, if Colter *was* willing to talk, David wanted to listen.

He put in a call to Sergeant Packer, but was told he'd stepped away from his desk for a minute. David left his name and number and a message for Packer to call him as soon as possible.

Then he went around the house to the garages, got into his Thunderbird, and drove off.

BRADLEE'S FATHER DIDN'T seem surprised that she was leaving town.

"That's probably for the best, darlin'," he said, ordering them both a drink.

It was a little early in the day for Bradlee, but when the waiter set her glass of wine in front of her, she took a sip and grimaced.

"Where's Crystal today?"

"She's out shopping with a friend." Her father glanced away, looking guilty.

"Dad, is there something you're not telling me?"

Her father sighed. "Never could hide anything from you, could I, darlin'? You're like your mother in that regard."

"So out with it," Bradlee said.

"Crystal's with Rachel Hollingsworth."

Bradlee's mouth dropped open. "Crystal knows Rachel?"

"Not exactly. I mean, she does now." He ran a hand through his hair. "I'm the one who called Rachel and told her about the party. Told her about you and David."

Bradlee couldn't have been more stunned. Or confused. *"Why?"*

He shrugged. "I thought it for the best. It seemed to me that boy was stringing you along while he had another one dancing on the line. I thought if I got his girl down here, she might straighten things out with him."

Bradlee shook her head. "How did you even know about her?"

His gaze lifted to meet Bradlee's. "You think Iris Kingsley is the only one who can hire a private investigator?"

"You had David *investigated?*" Bradlee's shock was fast turning into anger. "You had no right. None of this is any of your business."

"You're my business. I don't want to see you hurt, darlin'."

"Oh, don't 'darlin' me!" Bradlee retorted. "You've never taken any interest in my affairs before.'' Bad choice of words, she thought with a grimace, but nevertheless, she'd made her point.

He leaned toward her, folding his arms on the table. ''I know you're going to find this hard to believe, but I care about you, Bradlee. I want you to be happy. You've spent your entire life pining for that boy, and I thought if you could see for yourself that he hasn't exactly been waiting around for you, you'd wake up and face reality.''

''So you called Rachel. I suppose she was only too happy to oblige.''

Her father's face clouded. ''I may have gotten more than I bargained for with that one.''

''What do you mean?''

''Rachel Hollingsworth is not a woman I'd want on my bad side. I have to say, darlin', I think you're making a smart move getting the hell out of Dodge.''

WHEN BRADLEE ARRIVED back at the Kingsley estate, she still had several hours before her flight. The wine she'd had with her father—or perhaps the conversation—had left a sour feeling in her stomach, and the prospect of a long plane ride that evening was a bit daunting.

She met Illiana in the foyer. ''The house seems so quiet. Where is everyone?''

''Miss Pamela and Mr. Jeremy are out, Mr. Edward is in the library, and Mrs. Kingsley is upstairs resting.''

''What about Mr. Powers?''

''I saw him out in the gardens earlier.''

Bradlee nodded.

"Most of the staff are off this afternoon," Illiana said. "Can I get you anything?"

"No, thanks. I'm not feeling very well," Bradlee told her. "I think I'll go upstairs and rest."

"Very well. I'm taking off, then."

"Have a nice afternoon."

In her bedroom, Bradlee closed and locked the door. Her lack of sleep the previous night was starting to take its toll. She decided to lie down for a few minutes and take a brief nap. At least that way she wouldn't have to think about David, she thought drowsily.

But she dreamed about their lovemaking, and when she woke up, the hurt she'd been trying to keep at bay all day descended over her. She suddenly felt more depressed than she ever had before because she knew once she got on that plane, the chances were good she would never see David again.

Getting up, Bradlee started across the room to wash her face in the bathroom, but stopped when she saw that someone had shoved a note under her door. She picked it up and read:

Bradlee:
Illiana told me you weren't feeling well so I didn't want to disturb you in case you were sleeping. I think I've remembered something. I'm going back to the nursery to see if it'll help jog my memory. If you wake up in time and see

this note, please come find me. I need your help. I think this could be it.

It was signed "David." Not "Love, David," of course.

Still, he did say he needed her. Bradlee warned herself not to read more into those words than he actually meant, but excitement shot through her anyway. David needed her, but what's more, he'd remembered something. *"I think this could be it."*

Bradlee went into the bathroom and hurriedly washed her face and combed her hair. Slipping into her shoes, she let herself out of her room and headed toward the nursery.

By the time she got to that part of the house, her excitement had begun to fade. An uneasiness crept over her. What if David hadn't written that note? What if this was some sort of trap?

But who would be foolish enough to try something in broad daylight? The only people in the house besides her and David were Edward, who was probably in a drunken stupor by now, and Iris, whose strength seemed to be fading fast these days.

Still, Bradlee wasn't about to make the same mistake she'd made the night of the party. She wouldn't enter the nursery until she knew for sure David was in there.

Pausing in the hallway, Bradlee was just about to call out to him when a shadow appeared in the doorway. A scream of terror rose in Bradlee's throat.

DAVID HAD GOTTEN CAUGHT in a traffic jam due to road construction and hadn't even made it out of the city when his cell phone rang again.

"Hello?"

"Powers? This is Sergeant Packer."

"I'm glad you got my message," David said.

Packer hesitated. "Message? What message? I just got back in. Oh, wait a minute. Here it is."

David frowned. "That's not the reason you're calling?"

"No, I guess that's just what they call a happy coincidence. Actually, I thought you might want to know we turned up a match on some of the fresh prints we found in the nursery."

David felt a surge of adrenaline. He thought he knew exactly whose prints Packer had found. Jeremy Willows's. "Don't keep me in suspense, Sergeant."

"Are you sure you're ready for this?"

Something in his tone made David's heart thud against his chest.

"The prints belonged to Edward Kingsley. Can you believe that? His were still on file from when he was governor. It was a perfect match."

"Oh, my God," David said. Except for Iris, Bradlee was home alone with Edward. "Meet me at the Kingsley estate. Get over there as fast as you can."

BRADLEE STARED AT IRIS Kingsley in the nursery doorway. Her face was as white as Bradlee's felt. Iris put a hand to her heart, looking as if she was about to collapse.

Bradlee hurried over to her. "Are you all right?"

"My dear, you frightened me half to death. I wasn't expecting anyone to come up here."

"Isn't David here?"

"No, why?"

Bradlee's own heartbeat was almost back to normal, but she could see that Iris was still trembling. "I'm really sorry I frightened you, but David—or someone—left me a note asking me to meet him up here."

Iris's dark blue gaze met Bradlee's. Something that looked very much like fear flashed across her face. "That's very strange. David left the house some time ago. I saw him drive away myself."

Bradlee's voice sharpened. "Are you sure?"

"Yes, of course. His car is very distinctive."

Iris turned and walked back into the nursery. "Why do you suppose someone would send you a note pretending to be David?"

Bradlee lingered in the doorway. "To lure me up here, I'm afraid."

Iris turned. "But there's no one up here but me, and I've been here for some time. Perhaps I spoiled someone's plans."

"Let's hope so," Bradlee said. She glanced around the room. The blinds had been raised, and sunlight flooded into the room. It didn't look at all menacing today, but still, she wasn't about to get careless. "Perhaps we should go. It might not be safe up here."

For the first time, Bradlee saw a tea service had been placed on a table near the French doors. Iris sat down behind the table and lifted her teacup. "I'm not going anywhere until I finish my tea," she said calmly. She met Bradlee's gaze again and smiled. "I know what you're thinking. I'm a senile old woman, but there's a perfectly reasonable explanation for all this."

"There is?" Bradlee wasn't sure which "all this" Iris was referring to. The note? Or Iris having tea in an abandoned nursery?

"Every so often I come here and have tea with my grandsons. Oh, I know Andrew is dead, and Adam was missing and presumed dead for years, but this has always kept me close to both of them. Here in this room, my memories have always kept them alive for me, so I come here and sip my tea and let myself remember the happy days. I adored those boys. More than anything."

In the sunlight, a tear shimmered on Iris's cheek. "You must think me perfectly insane," she whispered.

Bradlee walked over to her. "Not at all. I can see how this room would keep drawing you back. It does me, too." She looked around, her gaze resting on the lone little bed. Adam's bed. Iris had kept this room just as it was, waiting for his return.

There was another cup on the tray, and Iris poured Bradlee some tea. "If anyone understands how I feel, it's you, my dear. You were always so close to Adam. You were as devastated as I was when he disappeared."

She handed the cup to Bradlee and stood. Walking

over to the French doors, she opened them and stepped out onto the balcony.

Bradlee said quickly, "I don't think it's a good idea to be out there. The railing hasn't been mended yet."

"I won't get close to the edge," Iris promised. She turned to stare at Bradlee in the doorway. "I used to sit out here for hours at a time with Adam and Andrew. I would read to them while they played at my feet. Those were the happiest days of my life. Then their mother got sick, and everything started to go wrong. Especially for Edward." A tear trickled down her cheek. "My son is...not well, I'm afraid. He hasn't been for years."

As she spoke, Iris seemed to grow physically weaker and she put a hand on the railing to steady herself. Alarmed, Bradlee stepped out onto the balcony and grabbed Iris's arm. "The railing is still broken. Don't lean against it. You need to come back inside."

Iris took a step away from the railing. "I'm all right," she said. "Please. Just let me finish my tea out here and then I promise I'll come back inside."

"All right," Bradlee agreed reluctantly. "But stay away from the edge."

Iris lifted her cup to her lips and sipped delicately. "It's Earl Grey. I brewed it myself—one of the few things I can still do. Do you like it?"

Bradlee took a tentative sip. "It's very good."

Iris sighed. "You're humoring me, of course. So

many people do that with me these days. The price of getting old and dying slowly, I'm afraid.''

"No, I mean it," Bradlee said. "It's really good." She took another sip, and Iris smiled.

"I've always liked you, Bradlee. If the circumstances were different, I wouldn't have minded seeing you and Adam together."

Circumstances? What was she talking about? Bradlee wondered. And why was she staring at her so curiously. "Is something wrong?"

Iris cocked her head slightly. "I was just about to ask you the same thing. Are you feeling all right?"

"Yes, I'm fine—" It hit her all at once. A great wave of dizziness rolled over Bradlee, and she gasped, stumbling backward. The teacup and saucer fell from her hands and shattered. Iris was hardly more than a blur to Bradlee.

She put out her hands beseechingly. "Help me—"

"I can't do that, Bradlee. I'm sorry, but if you'd stayed away, I wouldn't have to do this. But it's only a matter of time before you remember who you saw in the nursery that night, and I can't let that happen. I have a destiny to fulfill, you know. A place in history that I can't allow you to take away from me."

As she looked at Iris's face, hovering slightly above her, something suddenly became clear. Iris bending over Adam's crib... Iris putting a cloth over his face. *He can't breathe!* she'd wanted to scream at Iris, but she'd been too frightened. She had watched as Iris moved across the room to the French doors, opened them, and waved to someone waiting in the shadows below. Then Iris had come back into the room. Slowly she'd crossed the room to Bradlee's bed. Bradlee had squeezed her eyes closed, but it was too late. Iris had seen that she was awake, and before Bradlee could utter a sound, Iris had shoved a pillow over her face and held it fast.

Can't breathe!

"You tried...to kill me," Bradlee gasped. "Smother...me."

"I'd knew you'd seen me," Iris said. "I had to frighten you enough to make sure you wouldn't talk. Or if you did, that your story would sound so fantastic, no one would believe you. And it worked. You were so traumatized you didn't utter a word for days. Then when you did speak, you rambled on about shadows. When your mother decided to take you to see a psychiatrist, I made sure to give her Dr. Scott's name. She owed me a favor, you see. She was one of the many underprivileged kids I'd sponsored through college—in her case, medical school. She wouldn't have dared refuse me."

"Why?" Bradlee whispered. Her head spun out of control. She wasn't sure how much longer she could remain on her feet. She had to get away from the railing. If she fell against it—

Iris moved between her and the French doors, blocking Bradlee's only means of escape. "Edward was losing," Iris said. "And Kingsleys never lose. Our family has always been a force in politics. I didn't want that to end. Not because of some stupid weakness Edward had for that woman."

Bradlee stumbled against the railing, felt it move beneath her weight.

"So I made a deal with Raymond Colter. He would kidnap Adam and then after the ransom money was paid, he would return my grandson unharmed. But it didn't work out that way. Adam wasn't returned to me, and I've had to live with that all these years. I couldn't even search for him, couldn't mount any kind of investigation, because Colter set it up to look like Adam was dead. And once that happened, my hands were tied. I could do nothing without giving myself away."

Bradlee could feel her knees buckling. "Please...help...me...." Iris reached out a hand toward her...and gave her a shove.

For an eternity, Bradlee wavered at the edge of the balcony, trying to regain her balance, but it was no use. She crashed backward into the railing, and for a split second, the remaining wood held. Then the railing splintered with a loud crack, and Bradlee fell through the opening.

DAVID CAME AROUND the corner of the house in time to see Bradlee hanging from the edge of the balcony. Her feet dangled precariously in midair, and for a split second, his heart completely stopped. He didn't waste time trying the rear entrance. The front door had been locked and bolted, as had the French doors to the library and study.

He used the trellis, the same way his kidnapper had gained entrance to the house thirty-two years ago and the same way Bradlee had escaped two nights ago. Thorns tore at his arms and hands, but David never felt the pain. His entire focus was on Bradlee, on reaching her before she fell.

When he was within five or six feet of her, he said her name softly, so as not to alarm her. "Hold on," he said. "I'm coming."

She didn't say anything, and David was glad she was conserving her energy. Her hold on the edge of the balcony was precarious at best. Within seconds, David had reached the balcony and climbed over the broken railing. He knelt and grabbed Bradlee's arms.

"Let go," he said. "I'll pull you up."

He wasn't even sure she heard him. With a tiny cry of terror, her fingers slid loose and for a moment, he thought she was going to slip from his grasp. He tightened his grip, and heaved her upward, until she was sprawled on the balcony beside him.

"It's okay. You're safe." He held her to him, not wanting to let her go. Not wanting to think how close he'd come to losing her.

"Iris—" she whispered.

"What about her?"

She looked dazed, but her eyes seemed to focus on something behind him. David turned and saw that his grandmother was standing just inside the nursery, holding a gun on them.

"Adam," she admonished. "I didn't want it to be this way. You weren't supposed to come back so soon. I could have had everything taken care of if you'd gone to see Raymond like you were supposed to.''

David's heart slammed against his chest. It was all clear now. Iris had tried to kill Bradlee, and she'd paid Raymond Colter to kidnap him all those years ago.

The secret was finally out.

''I know what you must be thinking,'' she said sadly. ''Why you, and not Andrew? I'm sorry you had to be the one. I loved you, Adam, more than you could ever know. But Andrew...Andrew was my heart. I couldn't let him go.''

''I understand,'' David said softly. ''Just put the gun down and let's talk about this.''

Her hand was trembling, but David knew she still had enough strength to pull the trigger. And the gun was now aimed at Bradlee.

Iris's eyes grew steely with resolve. ''Move away from her, Adam. Please. With her out of the way, no one will ever know. Now that you're home, we can be a real family again. I can give you everything. Power beyond your wildest dreams. Just move away from her, Adam. Please.''

''You'll have to kill me first,'' David said.

''And me,'' said another voice from inside the nursery.

Iris spun away from the French doors, but she didn't lower the gun. Edward moved into the room so that she could see him.

''Mother, you did this?'' he said in a hoarse whisper. "You took my son from me? You took my life from me? How could you?"

"I did it *for* you," Iris said. "Your obsession with that woman nearly ruined everything. If it wasn't for me, you never would have been elected governor."

"I wanted to pull out of the race when Adam was kidnapped," he said numbly. "But you talked me out of it. You said some good should come from such a terrible tragedy, and then when the body was recovered, when we thought Adam was dead, you said if I quit, my son would have died in vain. So I ran and I won, but I couldn't live with myself. I couldn't forgive myself for profiting from my own son's death. All those years you let me think him dead. You watched me destroy myself out of grief and guilt, when all along it was *you*."

"Edward, please. Think of our good name. The Kingsley reputation—"

Edward walked slowly toward her. "That's exactly what I *am* thinking about. How far you were willing to go to keep your precious power. But it's over now, Mother. It's all over."

"No! I won't let it be. There's still time—"

"What are you going to do?" Edward demanded. "Shoot us all? That would be a little hard for even a Kingsley to talk her way out of. It's over, Mother. Drop the gun."

For a moment, Iris seemed to waver, and then slowly the gun lowered to her side and slipped from her fingers to the floor. She walked out of the nursery without looking back.

David helped Bradlee to her feet. The effects of the drug were starting to wear off—or maybe the terror of the near fall had helped clear her head. She leaned into David as they walked into the nursery.

Edward stood watching them. His gaze fell on David and he shook his head. "I've come into this room every night for over thirty years and prayed that wherever you were, you somehow knew I loved you. I would have moved heaven and earth to find you. I never knew what she did, but I should have. *Somehow* I should have known. I don't know how I can ever make it up to you. How you can ever forgive me?"

"You just saved my life," David said hoarsely. "I don't know what more a son could ask of his father."

Tears streaming down his face, Edward put his arms around David and held him as if he were three years old again.

IRIS KINGSLEY'S FUNERAL took place three days later at Saint Mary's, an elegant old cathedral in downtown Memphis where she and her husband had been married, and where her twin grandsons had been christened. Dignitaries from all over the country turned out en masse to mourn the passing of a political legend.

The doctor who had been summoned to Iris's deathbed the same day she'd tried to kill Bradlee declared that her death was from natural causes. Her heart had simply worn out.

But he hadn't known about the empty bottle of

sleeping pills David and Bradlee had found by her bedside—the same pills Iris had used to drug Bradlee. What was the point of making it public? Edward had suffered enough, and Iris's coconspirator was behind bars for the rest of his life. It was time for the past to be laid to rest.

After the service, David and Bradlee rode home in the limousine with Edward. Pamela and Jeremy left in a separate car and would not be returning to the mansion. The day after his mother died, Edward had asked Pamela for a divorce, and surprisingly, she hadn't put up a fuss. Both she and Jeremy had moved out that same night, and Edward hadn't had a drink since.

When they arrived home, he said, "I'm going up to rest for a while. Why don't you two get out of this gloomy house. It's a beautiful day."

"He's right," David said, taking Bradlee's hand. The two of them hadn't had much of a chance to talk the last three days. There had been a million details to take care of.

They walked out into the gardens and found a bench in the sunshine. September was coming to an end, and in the late afternoon, there was a definite chill in the air.

Bradlee sighed deeply. "I feel as if I've been on an emotional roller coaster for days. I'm drained."

"I know what you mean," David said. He put an arm around her shoulder and drew her close. Bradlee resisted for only a moment.

Sensing her reluctance, he glanced down at her.

"About the other night...you do understand why I said the things I did, don't you? I wanted you to leave town because I was worried about you, Bradlee. I was afraid for you."

She drew a long breath. "You were so convincing. I thought for sure that—"

"I know. Because that's what I wanted you to think. But that night was as special for me as it was for you." He stared down at her tenderly. "The earth did move, I swear it."

Her eyes glistened. "You don't know how much I want to believe you."

"Then let me prove it to you." His gaze softened, making Bradlee feel all weak and trembly inside. He put both arms around her and murmured against her ear, "I love you. I love you. I love you."

A tear spilled over and ran down her cheek. "I've waited so long to hear you say that."

He thumbed away her tears. "I think I'm beginning to realize that. The question now is, what do we do about it?"

"What do you mean?"

"I mean, we live on separate coasts, Bradlee. Where do we go from here?"

"Do I give up my career and move to New York with you, or do you give up your career and move to L.A. with me?"

"Exactly," he replied. "Or do we strike a happy medium, and both move back here to Memphis?"

Bradlee stared up at him in surprise. "You want to move back to Memphis?"

He shrugged. "I think we're both still Southerners at heart. Besides, I would like to get to know…my father. But it would mean both of us giving up our careers and starting all over. That's a lot to ask."

She thought about that for a moment. It wasn't such a difficult decision after all. There was only one place in the world that was home to her, and that was wherever David was. "You know, of course, you wouldn't have to work another day of your life if you didn't want to. Except for a generous trust fund for Edward, Iris left the entire Kingsley estate to you."

David's eyes darkened as he glanced over his shoulder at the mansion. "I grew up in a tiny two-bedroom house," he said. "I went to college on a scholarship and worked as a janitor in a high school to put myself through law school. That life is still more real to me than all of this."

"Having money doesn't have to be bad, you know. Power doesn't have to corrupt. You could do a lot of good with your inheritance, David. Think how many kids you could help go to college."

"Maybe you're right," he murmured, his lips in her hair. For a long moment, they were silent, then he said, "Don't you think we'd better get started?"

"You mean get back to the house?"

"I mean on that houseful of kids you always wanted. We're not getting any younger, Bradlee. But then, twins *do* run in my family."

Her heart began a slow, painful thudding in her chest. "Are you asking me to marry you?"

"That's the best way to have kids, I think."

"Are you sure you want to do this, David?"

He took her hands in his, skimming her fingers across his lips. "You told me once you'd been waiting all these years for me to come home. I think in some fundamental way, I was waiting for that, too. I don't know how or why, but you and I have always been connected, Bradlee. We always will be."

Her smile trembled as she stared up at him. "It's called destiny," she whispered, as he bent and touched his lips to hers.

Bradlee melted into the kiss, knowing in her heart that this was good. This was right. She and David were meant to be together.

After thirty-two years, they'd both finally found their way back home.

The three McCullar brothers once stood strong against the lawlessness on their ranches. Then the events of one fateful night shattered their bond and sent them far from home. But their hearts remained with the ranch—and the women—they left behind. And now all three are coming

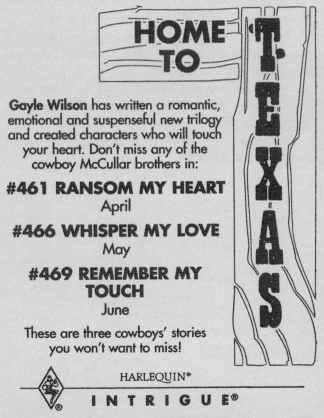

HOME TO
TEXAS

Gayle Wilson has written a romantic, emotional and suspenseful new trilogy and created characters who will touch your heart. Don't miss any of the cowboy McCullar brothers in:

#461 RANSOM MY HEART
April

#466 WHISPER MY LOVE
May

#469 REMEMBER MY TOUCH
June

These are three cowboys' stories you won't want to miss!

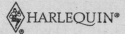

Not The Same Old Story!

Exciting, glamorous romance stories that take readers around the world.

Sparkling, fresh and tender love stories that bring you pure romance.

HARLEQUIN
Temptation.
Bold and adventurous— Temptation is strong women, bad boys, great sex!

HARLEQUIN SUPERROMANCE®
Provocative and realistic stories that celebrate life and love.

Contemporary fairy tales—where anything is possible and where dreams come true.

HARLEQUIN®
INTRIGUE®
Heart-stopping, suspenseful adventures that combine the best of romance and mystery.

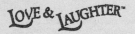
Humorous and romantic stories that capture the lighter side of love.

Catch more great

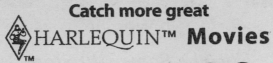 HARLEQUIN™ **Movies**

featured on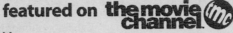

Premiering April 11th
Hard to Forget
based on the novel by bestselling
Harlequin Superromance® author
Evelyn A. Crowe

Don't miss next month's movie!
Premiering May 9th
The Awakening
starring Cynthia Geary and David Beecroft
based on the novel by Patricia Coughlin

If you are not currently a subscriber to
The Movie Channel, simply call your
local cable or satellite provider for more
details. Call today, and don't miss out
on the romance!

 HARLEQUIN™
Makes any time special.™

100% pure movies.
100% pure fun.